SUPERMAN®

FAMILY ADVENTURES™

STONE ARCH BOOKS
a capstone imprint

▼▼ STONE ARCH BOOKS™

Published in 2013
A Capstone Imprint
1710 Roe Crest Drive
North Mankato, MN 56003
www.capstonepub.com

Originally published by DC Comics in the U.S. in single
magazine form as SUPERMAN FAMILY ADVENTURES #6.
Copyright © 2013 DC Comics. All Rights Reserved.

DC Comics
1700 Broadway, New York, NY 10019
A Warner Bros. Entertainment Company

Cataloging-in-Publication Data is available at the
Library of Congress website:
ISBN: 978-1-4342-4794-0 (library binding)

Summary: Can it be true? Has Superman met his match in Metallo?
Who is Metallo? And what's up with his heart? Where does Lex Luthor
fit into all of this? Watch out! There's a new Super Hero in town!

STONE ARCH BOOKS
Ashley C. Andersen Zantop Publisher
Michael Dahl Editorial Director
Donald Lemke Editor
Brann Garvey Designer
Kathy McColley Production Specialist

DC COMICS
Kristy Quinn Original U.S. Editor

Printed in China by Nordica.
0413/CA21300442
032013 007226NORDF13

SUPERMAN® FAMILY ADVENTURES™

THE MENACE OF METALLO!

by Art Baltazar & Franco

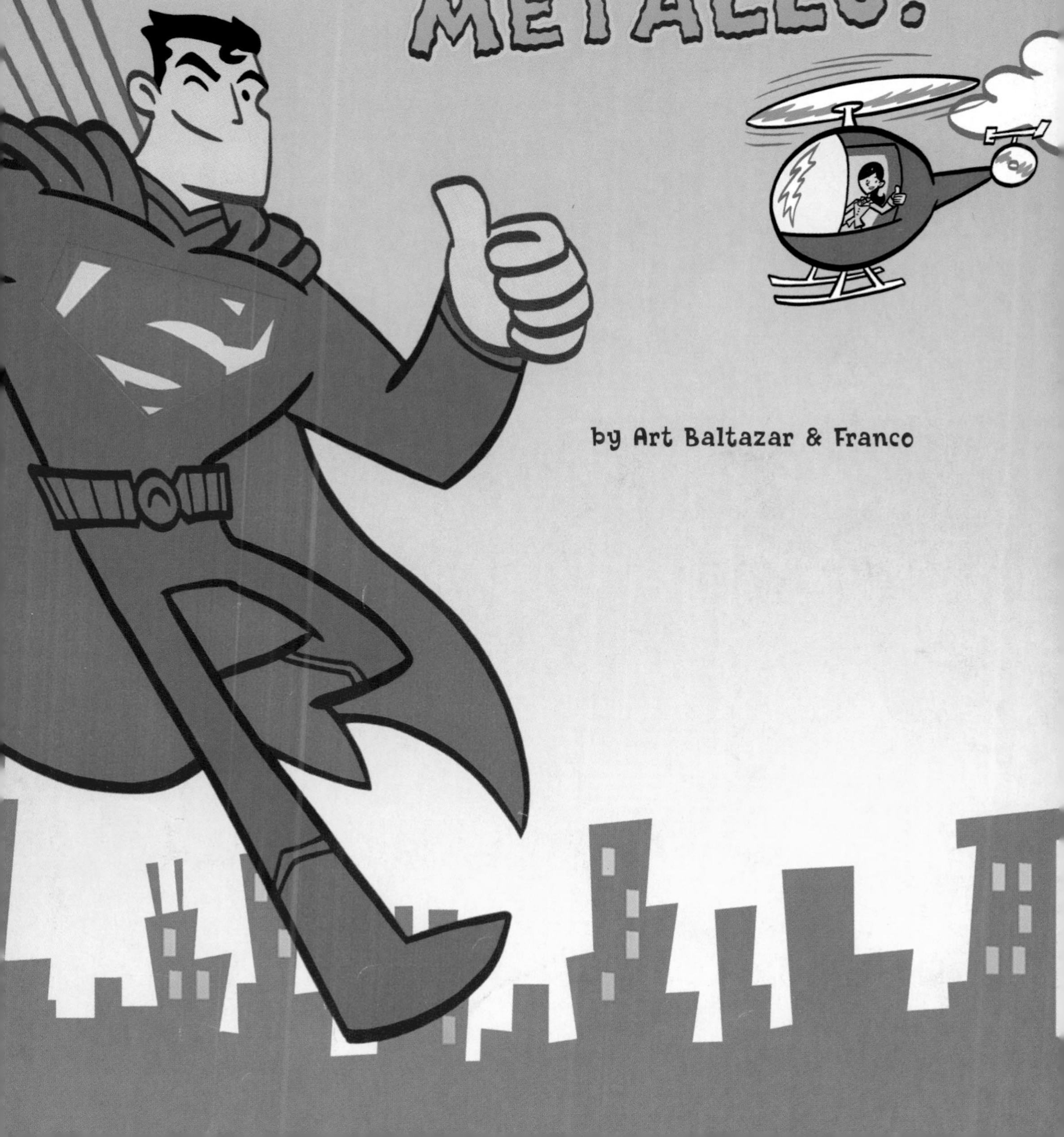

SUPERMAN® FAMILY ADVENTURES™

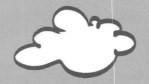

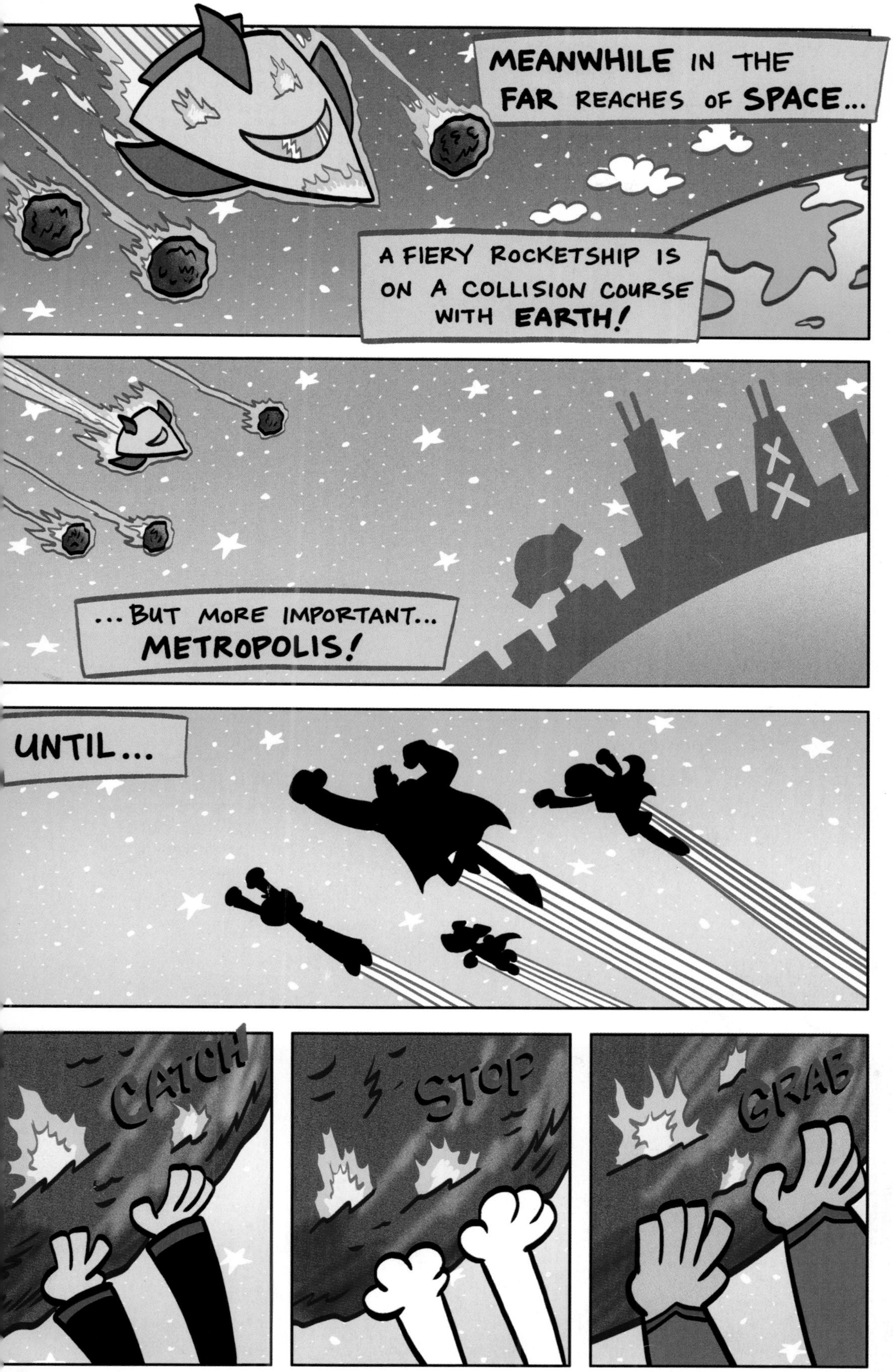
MEANWHILE IN THE FAR REACHES OF SPACE...
A FIERY ROCKETSHIP IS ON A COLLISION COURSE WITH EARTH!
...BUT MORE IMPORTANT... METROPOLIS!
UNTIL...
CATCH
STOP
GRAB

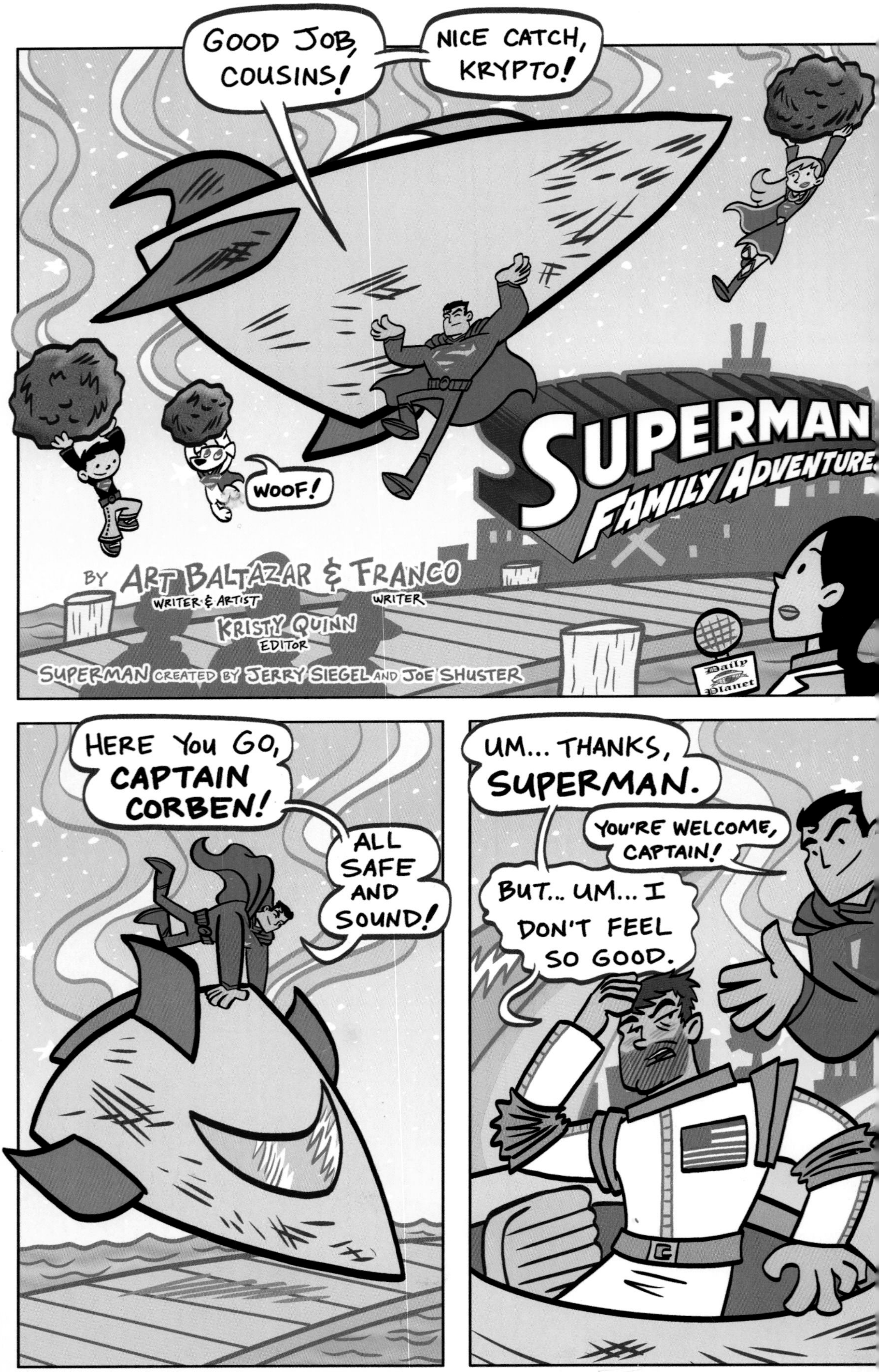
GOOD JOB, COUSINS!
NICE CATCH, KRYPTO!
WOOF!
SUPERMAN
FAMILY ADVENTURES
BY ART BALTAZAR & FRANCO
WRITER & ARTIST
WRITER
KRISTY QUINN
EDITOR
SUPERMAN CREATED BY JERRY SIEGEL AND JOE SHUSTER
Daily Planet
HERE YOU GO, CAPTAIN CORBEN!
ALL SAFE AND SOUND!
UM... THANKS, SUPERMAN.
YOU'RE WELCOME, CAPTAIN!
BUT... UM... I DON'T FEEL SO GOOD.

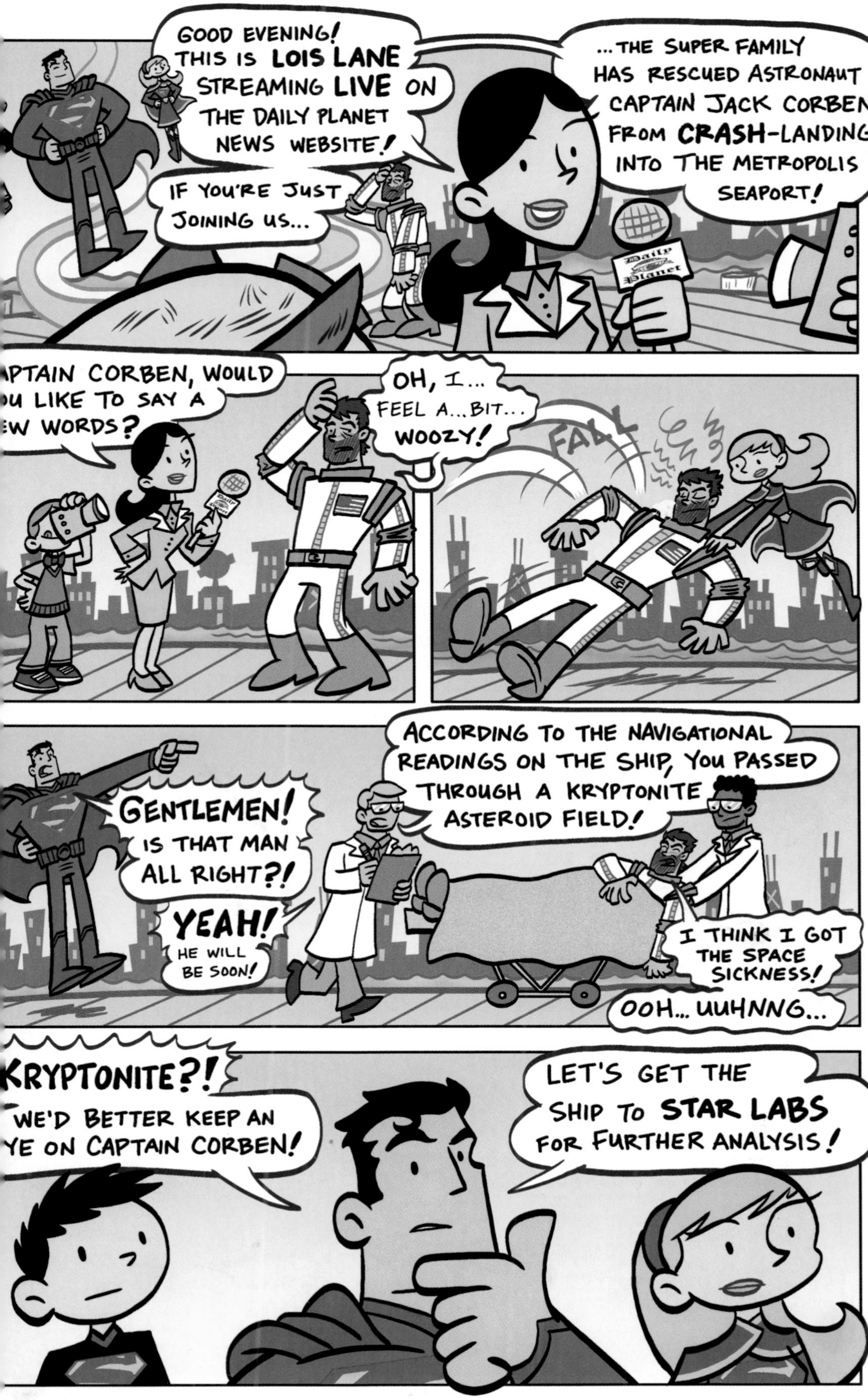
GOOD EVENING! THIS IS LOIS LANE STREAMING LIVE ON THE DAILY PLANET NEWS WEBSITE!
IF YOU'RE JUST JOINING US...
...THE SUPER FAMILY HAS RESCUED ASTRONAUT CAPTAIN JACK CORBEN FROM CRASH-LANDING INTO THE METROPOLIS SEAPORT!
Daily Planet
APTAIN CORBEN, WOULD OU LIKE TO SAY A EW WORDS?
OH, I... FEEL A... BIT... WOOZY!
FALL
GENTLEMEN! IS THAT MAN ALL RIGHT?!
YEAH! HE WILL BE SOON!
ACCORDING TO THE NAVIGATIONAL READINGS ON THE SHIP, YOU PASSED THROUGH A KRYPTONITE ASTEROID FIELD!
I THINK I GOT THE SPACE SICKNESS!
OOH... UUHNNG...
KRYPTONITE?! WE'D BETTER KEEP AN YE ON CAPTAIN CORBEN!
LET'S GET THE SHIP TO STAR LABS FOR FURTHER ANALYSIS!

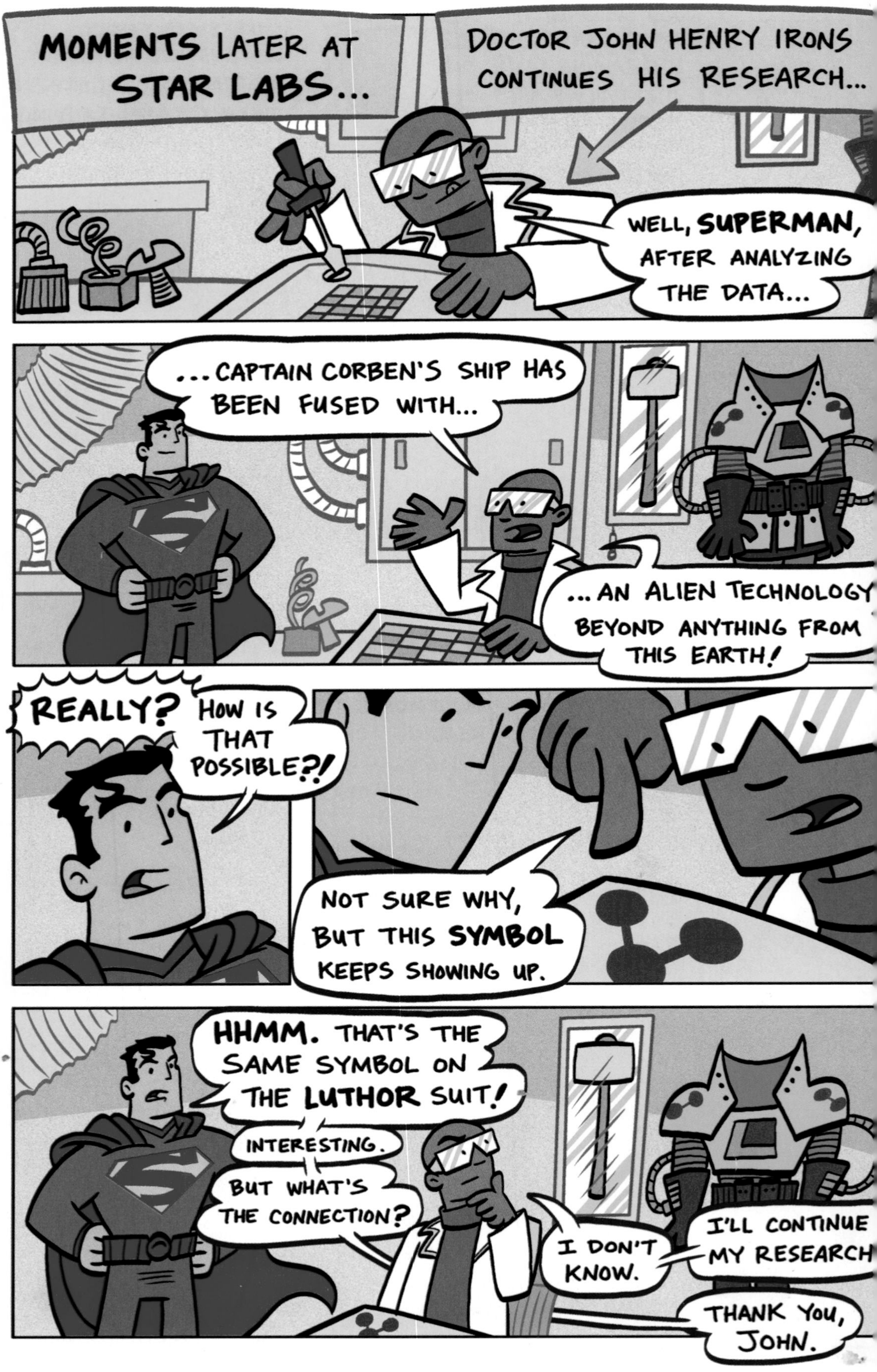
MOMENTS LATER AT STAR LABS...
DOCTOR JOHN HENRY IRONS CONTINUES HIS RESEARCH...
WELL, SUPERMAN, AFTER ANALYZING THE DATA...
...CAPTAIN CORBEN'S SHIP HAS BEEN FUSED WITH...
...AN ALIEN TECHNOLOGY BEYOND ANYTHING FROM THIS EARTH!
REALLY?
HOW IS THAT POSSIBLE?!
NOT SURE WHY, BUT THIS SYMBOL KEEPS SHOWING UP.
HHMM. THAT'S THE SAME SYMBOL ON THE LUTHOR SUIT!
INTERESTING.
BUT WHAT'S THE CONNECTION?
I DON'T KNOW.
I'LL CONTINUE MY RESEARCH.
THANK YOU, JOHN.

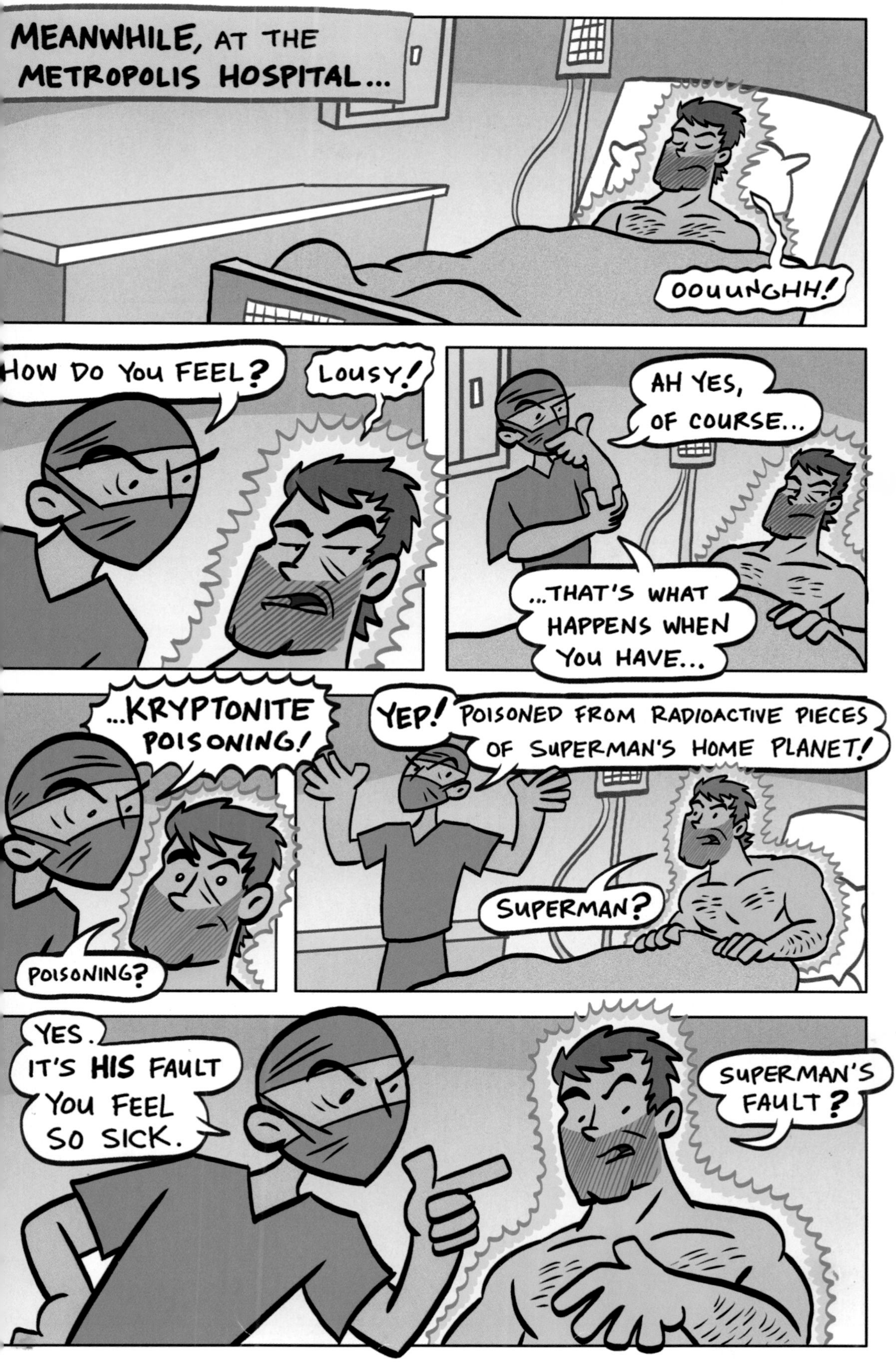
MEANWHILE, AT THE METROPOLIS HOSPITAL...
OOUUNGHH!
HOW DO YOU FEEL?
LOUSY!
AH YES, OF COURSE...
...THAT'S WHAT HAPPENS WHEN YOU HAVE...
...KRYPTONITE POISONING!
POISONING?
YEP!
POISONED FROM RADIOACTIVE PIECES OF SUPERMAN'S HOME PLANET!
SUPERMAN?
YES. IT'S HIS FAULT YOU FEEL SO SICK.
SUPERMAN'S FAULT?

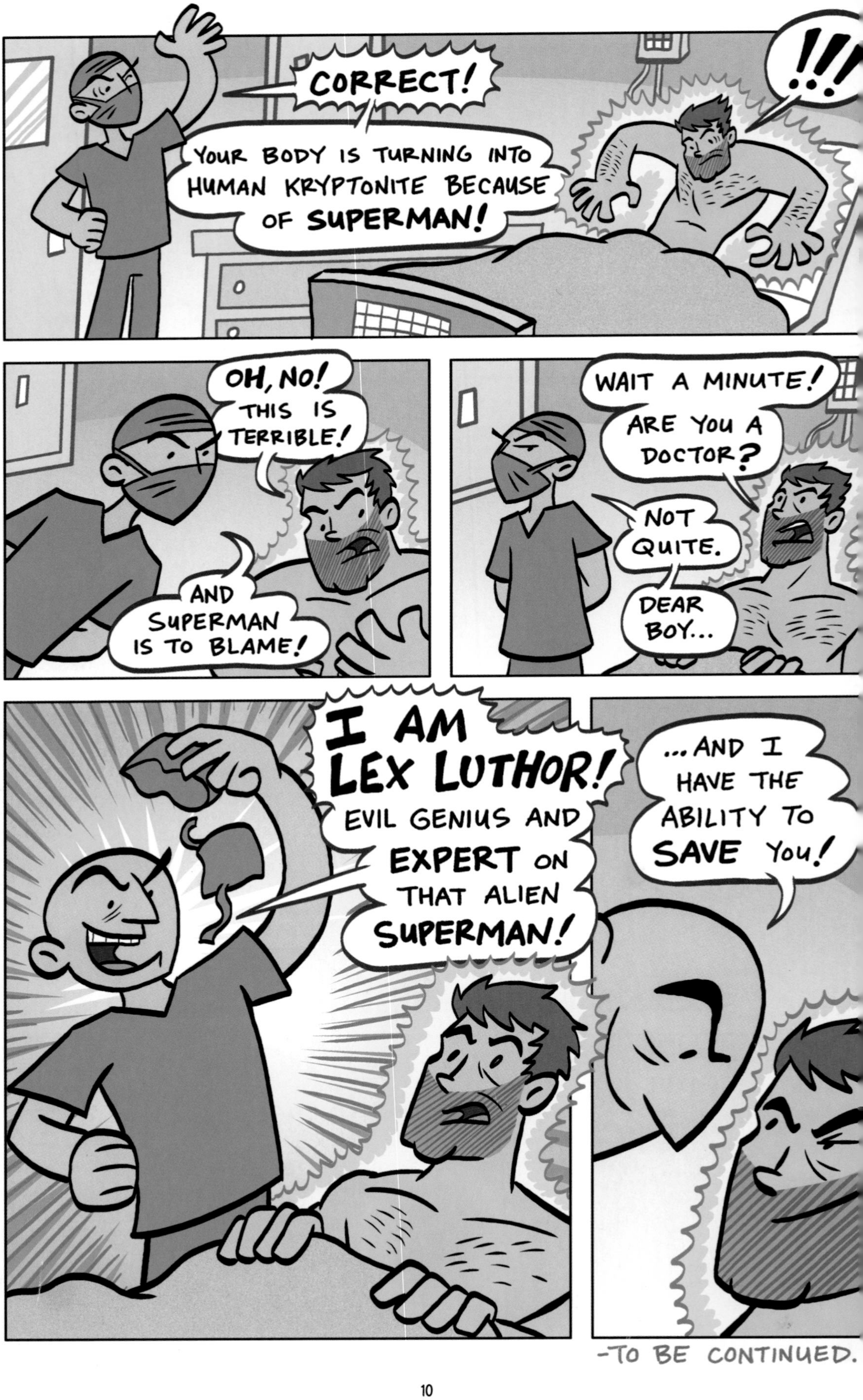
CORRECT!
YOUR BODY IS TURNING INTO HUMAN KRYPTONITE BECAUSE OF SUPERMAN!
!!!
OH, NO! THIS IS TERRIBLE!
AND SUPERMAN IS TO BLAME!
WAIT A MINUTE!
ARE YOU A DOCTOR?
NOT QUITE.
DEAR BOY...
I AM LEX LUTHOR! EVIL GENIUS AND EXPERT ON THAT ALIEN SUPERMAN!
...AND I HAVE THE ABILITY TO SAVE YOU!

-TO BE CONTINUED.

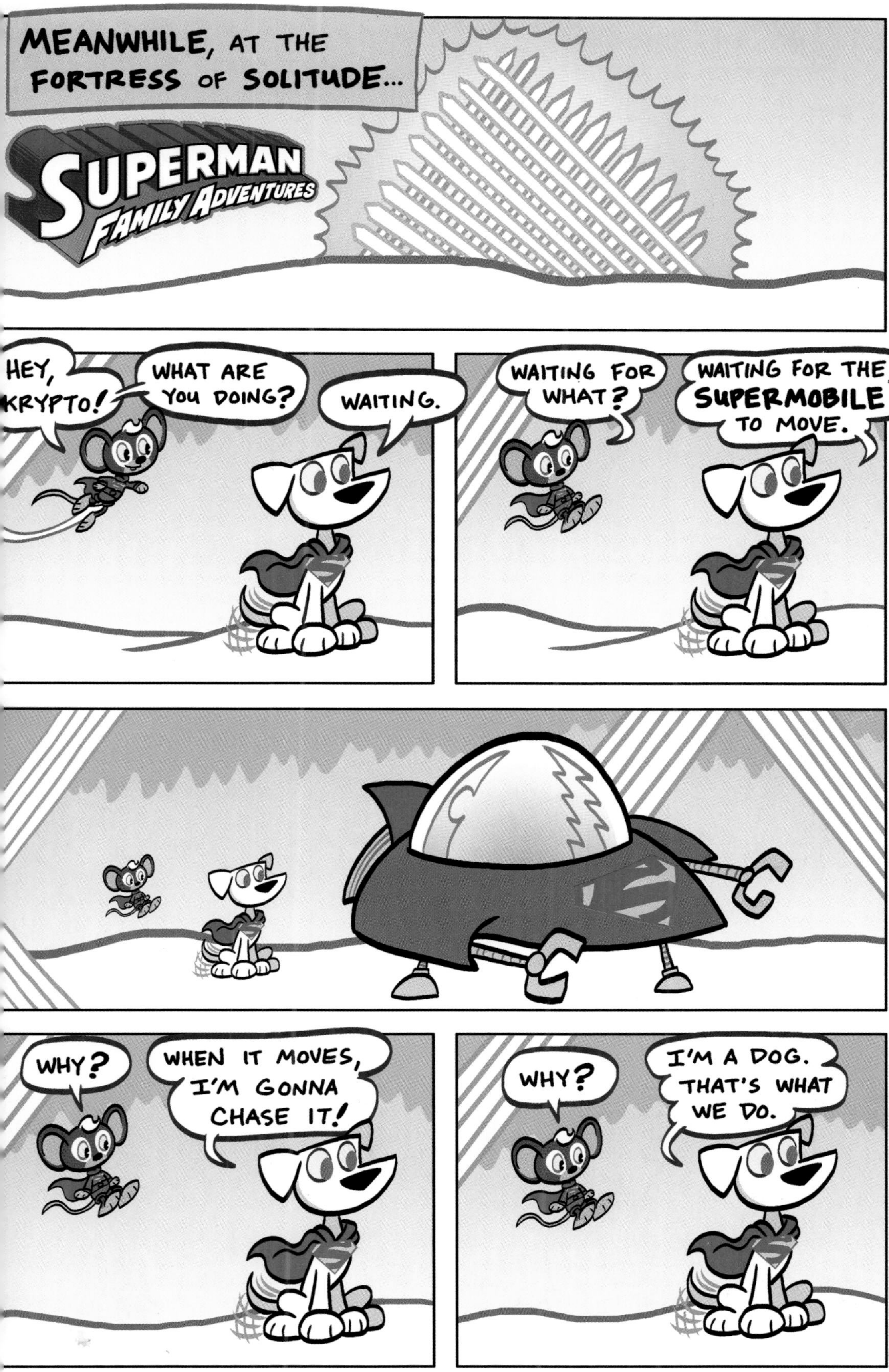
MEANWHILE, AT THE FORTRESS OF SOLITUDE...
SUPERMAN FAMILY ADVENTURES
HEY, KRYPTO!
WHAT ARE YOU DOING?
WAITING.
WAITING FOR WHAT?
WAITING FOR THE SUPERMOBILE TO MOVE.
WHY?
WHEN IT MOVES, I'M GONNA CHASE IT!
WHY?
I'M A DOG. THAT'S WHAT WE DO.

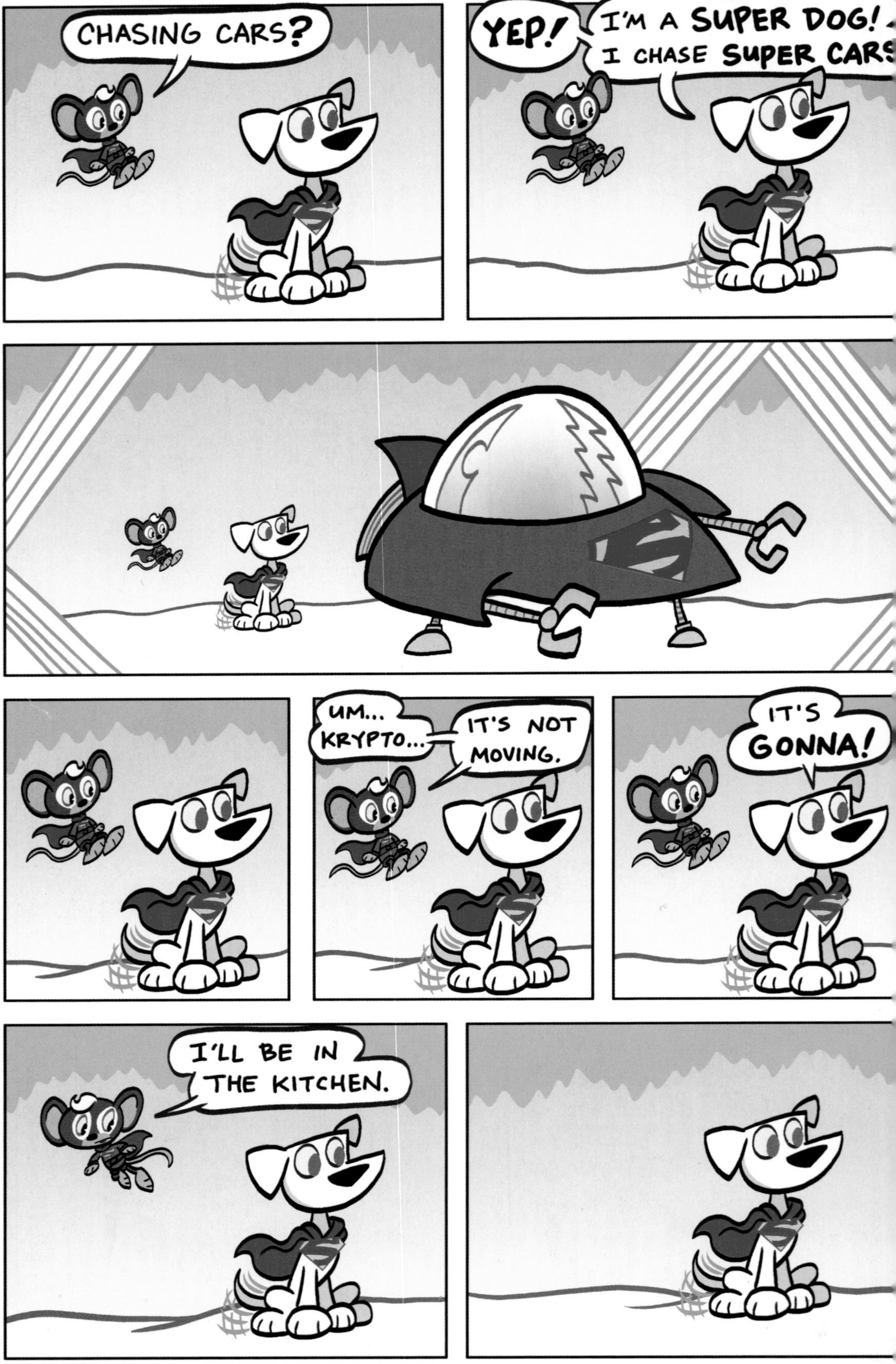
CHASING CARS?
YEP!
I'M A SUPER DOG!
I CHASE SUPER CARS
UM... KRYPTO...
IT'S NOT MOVING.
IT'S GONNA!
I'LL BE IN THE KITCHEN.

-AW YEAH ANTICIPATION!

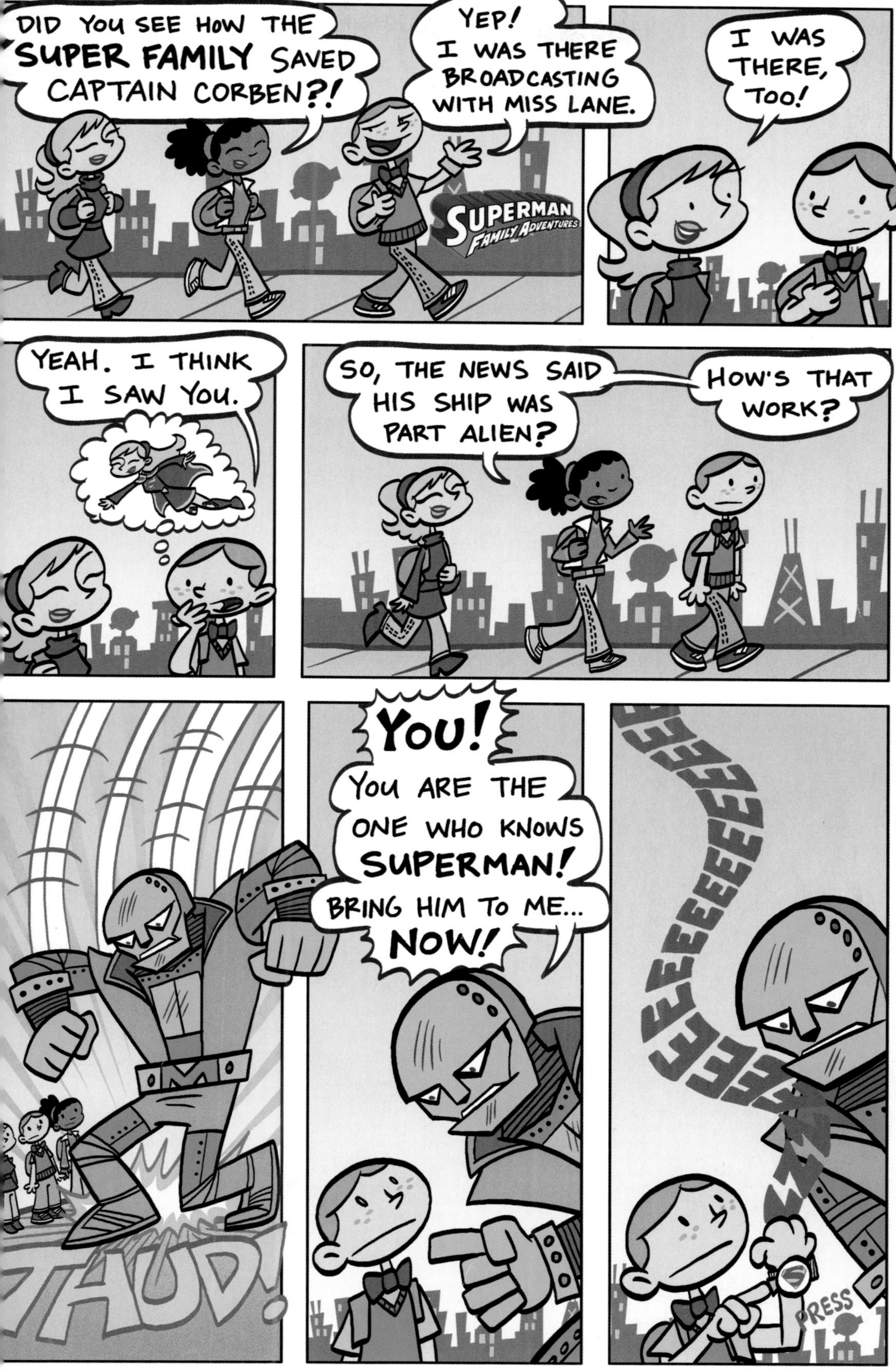
DID YOU SEE HOW THE SUPER FAMILY SAVED CAPTAIN CORBEN?!
YEP! I WAS THERE BROADCASTING WITH MISS LANE.
SUPERMAN FAMILY ADVENTURES
I WAS THERE, TOO!
YEAH. I THINK I SAW YOU.
SO, THE NEWS SAID HIS SHIP WAS PART ALIEN?
HOW'S THAT WORK?
THUD!
YOU!
YOU ARE THE ONE WHO KNOWS SUPERMAN!
BRING HIM TO ME... NOW!
EEEEEEEEEEEEEEEEEEEEEEEEEE
PRESS

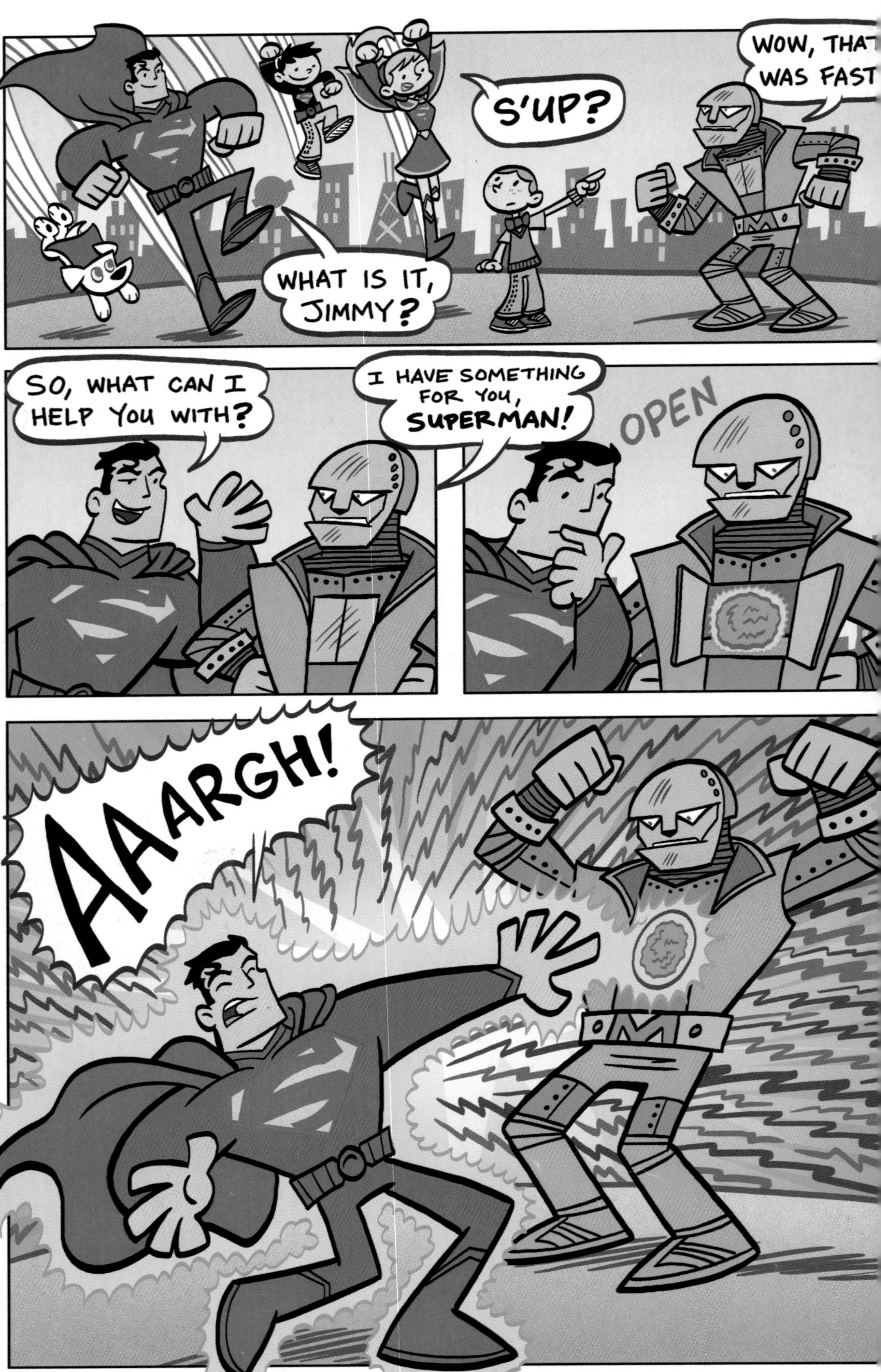
S'UP?
WOW, THAT
WAS FAST
WHAT IS IT, JIMMY?
SO, WHAT CAN I HELP YOU WITH?
I HAVE SOMETHING FOR YOU, SUPERMAN!
OPEN
AAARGH!

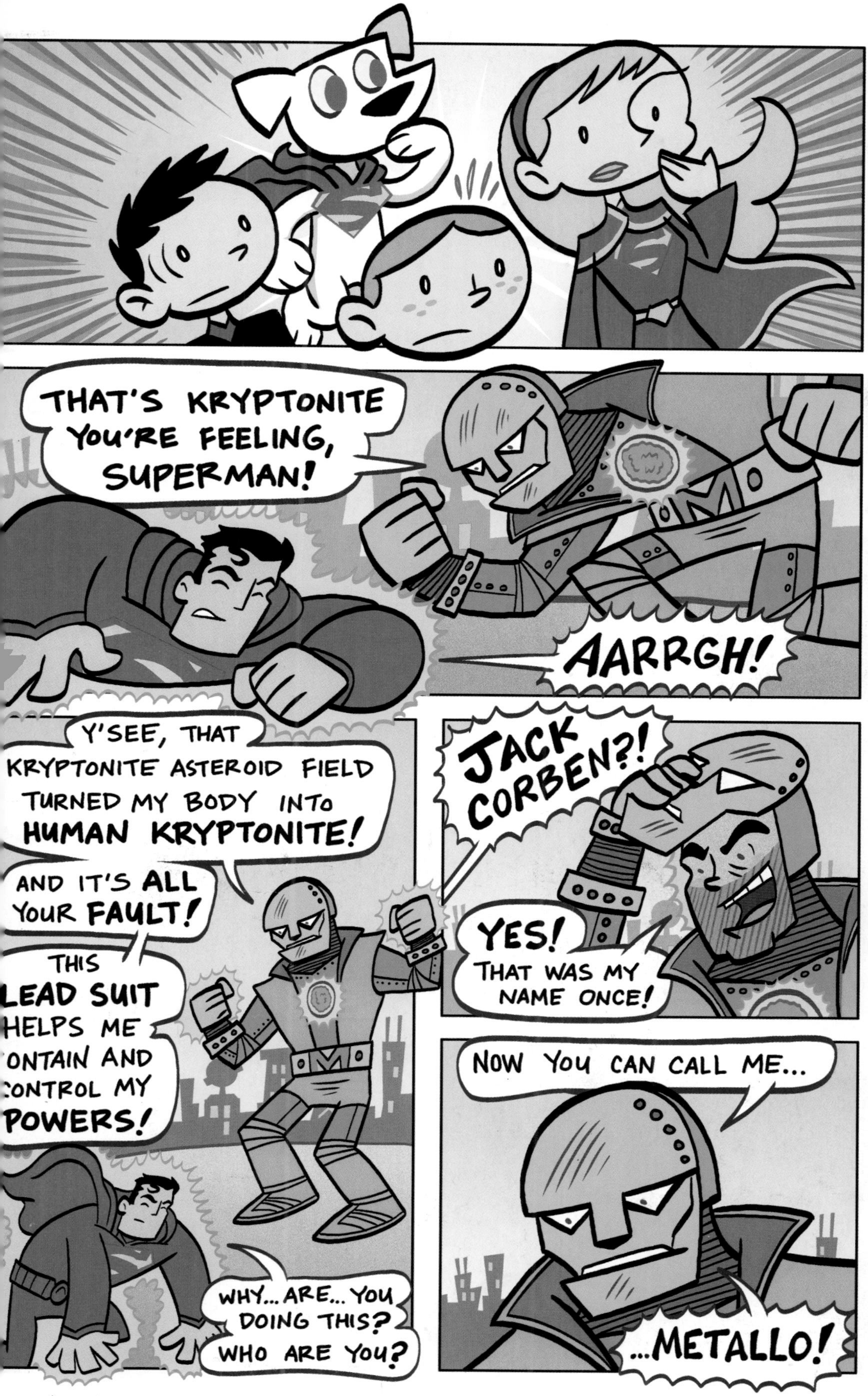
THAT'S KRYPTONITE YOU'RE FEELING, SUPERMAN!
AARRGH!
Y'SEE, THAT KRYPTONITE ASTEROID FIELD TURNED MY BODY INTO HUMAN KRYPTONITE!
AND IT'S ALL YOUR FAULT!
THIS LEAD SUIT HELPS ME CONTAIN AND CONTROL MY POWERS!
WHY... ARE... YOU DOING THIS? WHO ARE YOU?
JACK CORBEN?!
YES! THAT WAS MY NAME ONCE!
NOW YOU CAN CALL ME...
...METALLO!

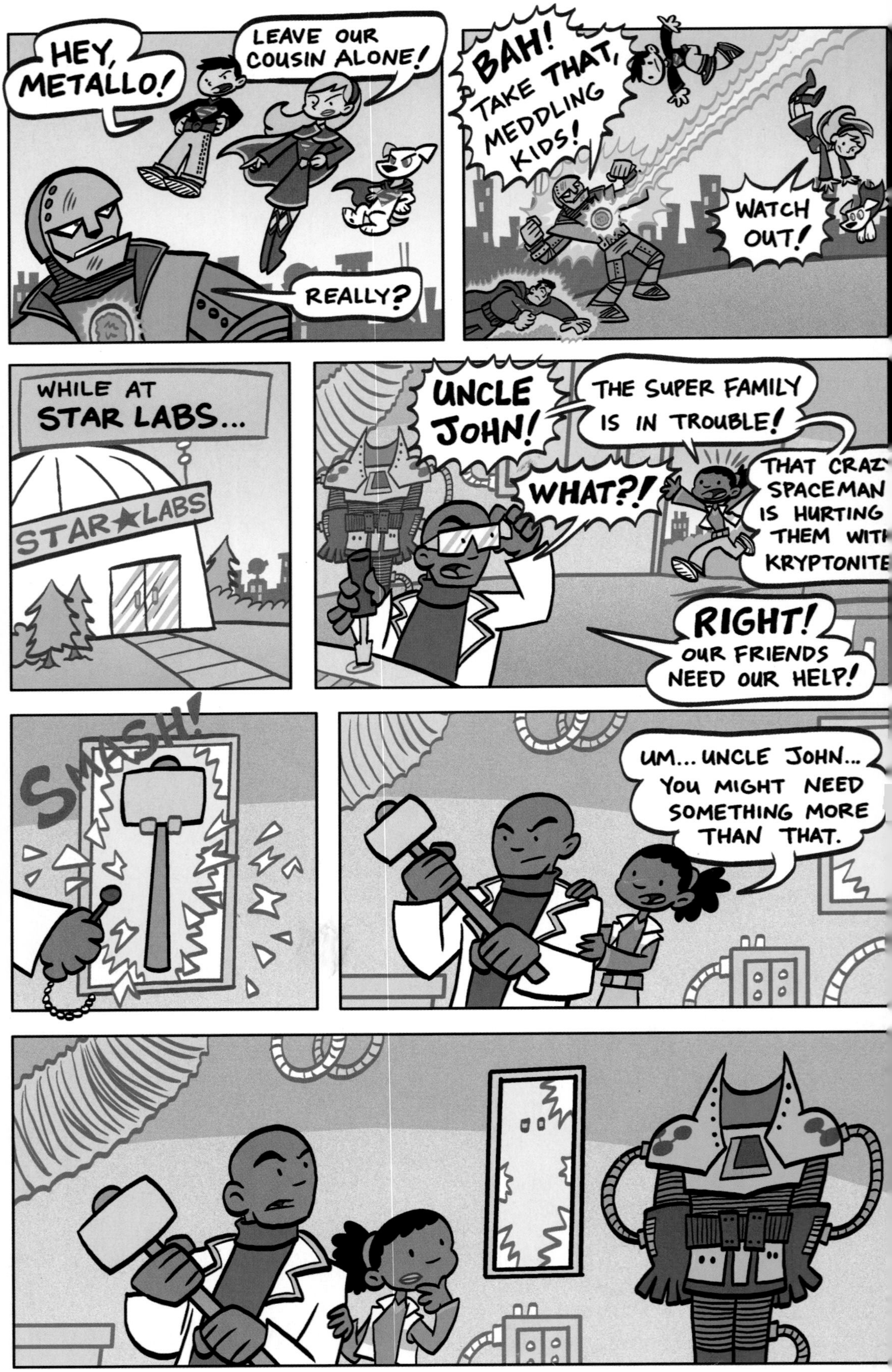

HEY, METALLO!
LEAVE OUR COUSIN ALONE!
REALLY?
BAH! TAKE THAT, MEDDLING KIDS!
WATCH OUT!
WHILE AT STAR LABS...
STAR★LABS
UNCLE JOHN!
THE SUPER FAMILY IS IN TROUBLE!
WHAT?!
THAT CRAZY SPACEMAN IS HURTING THEM WITH KRYPTONITE
RIGHT! OUR FRIENDS NEED OUR HELP!
SMASH!
UM... UNCLE JOHN... YOU MIGHT NEED SOMETHING MORE THAN THAT.

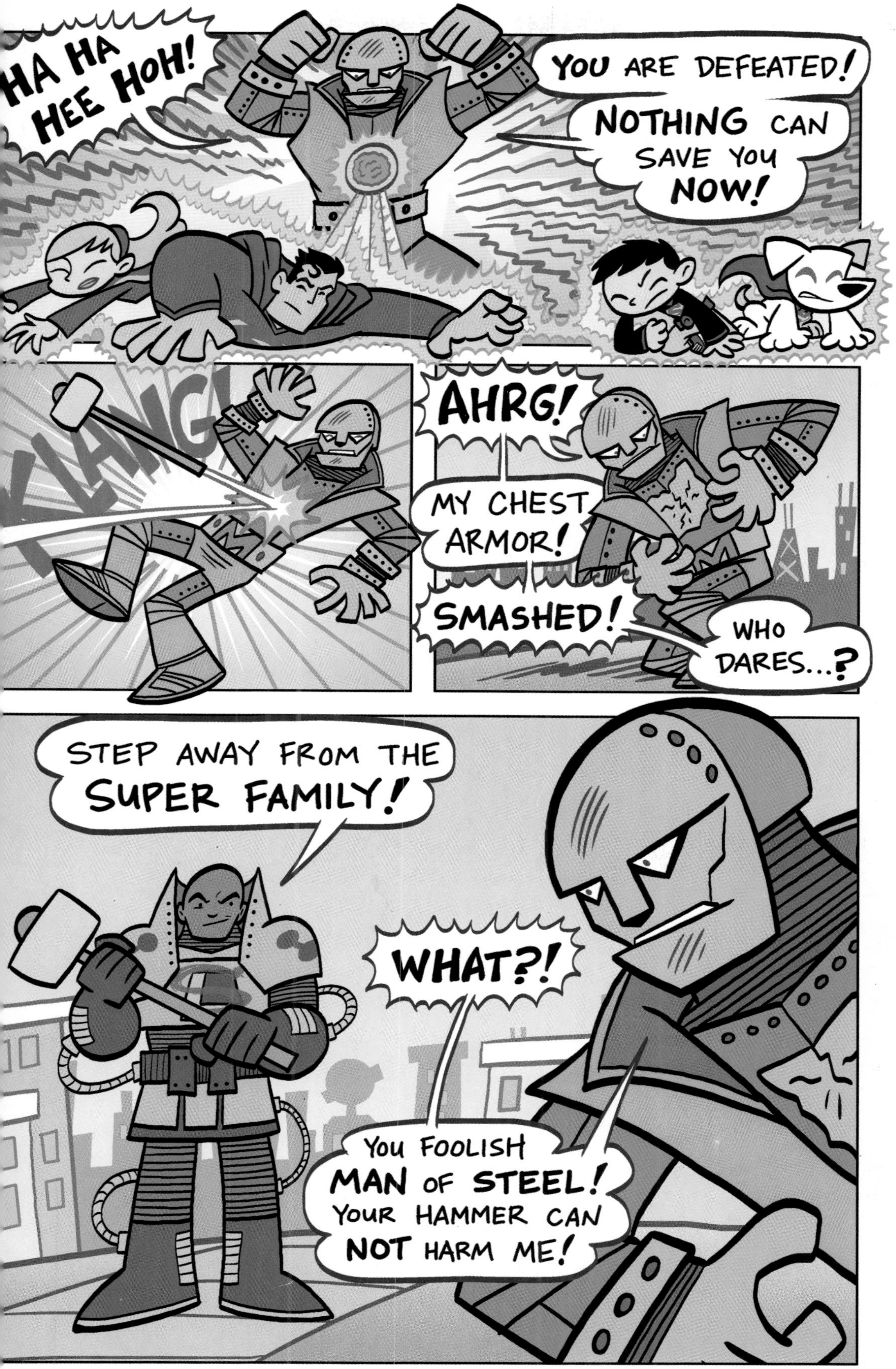
HA HA HEE HOH!
YOU ARE DEFEATED!
NOTHING CAN SAVE YOU NOW!
KLANG!
AHRG!
MY CHEST ARMOR!
SMASHED!
WHO DARES...?
STEP AWAY FROM THE SUPER FAMILY!
WHAT?!
YOU FOOLISH MAN OF STEEL! YOUR HAMMER CAN NOT HARM ME!

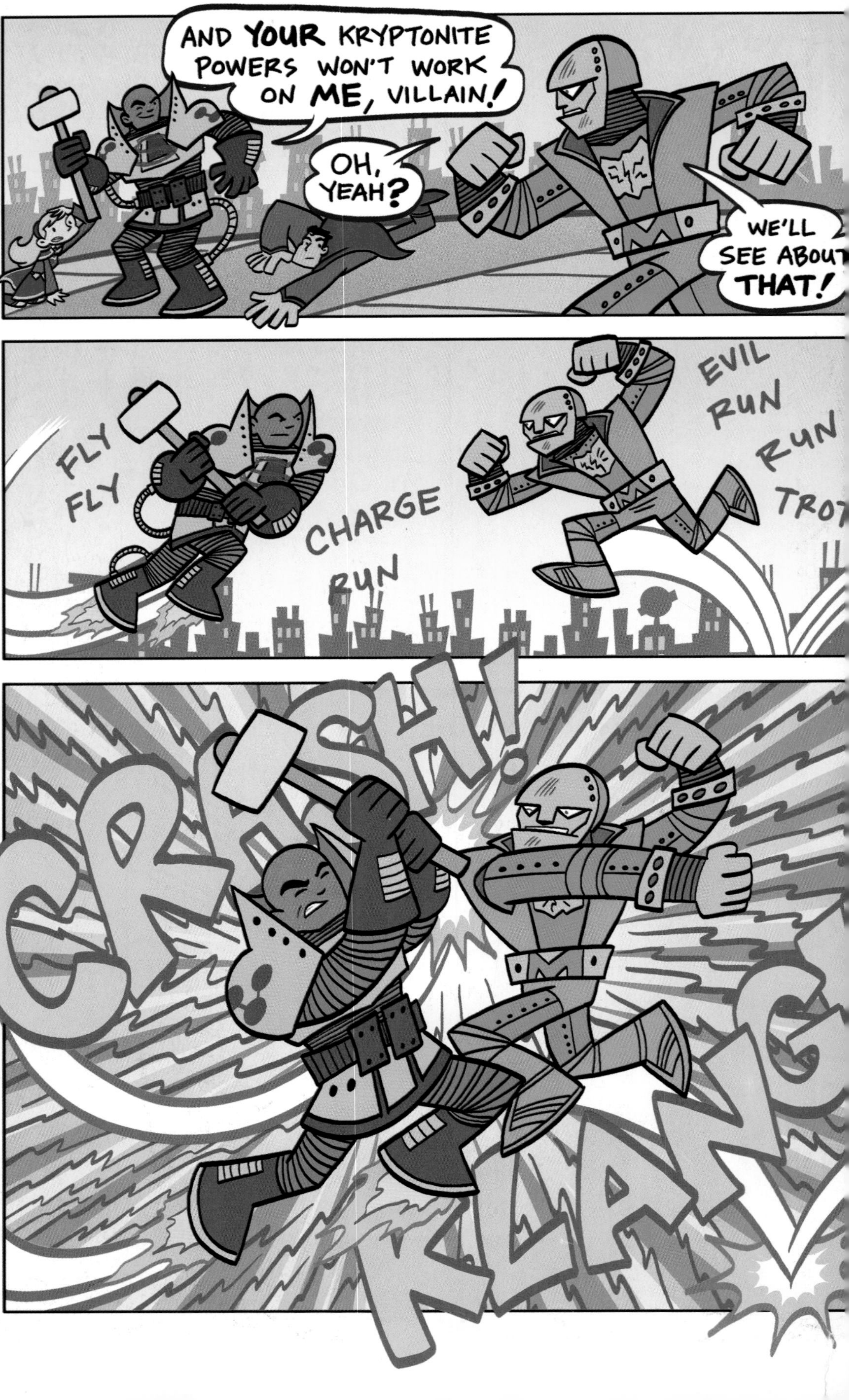
AND YOUR KRYPTONITE POWERS WON'T WORK ON ME, VILLAIN!
OH, YEAH?
WE'LL SEE ABOUT THAT!
FLY FLY
CHARGE RUN
EVIL RUN RUN TROT
CRASH!
KLANG

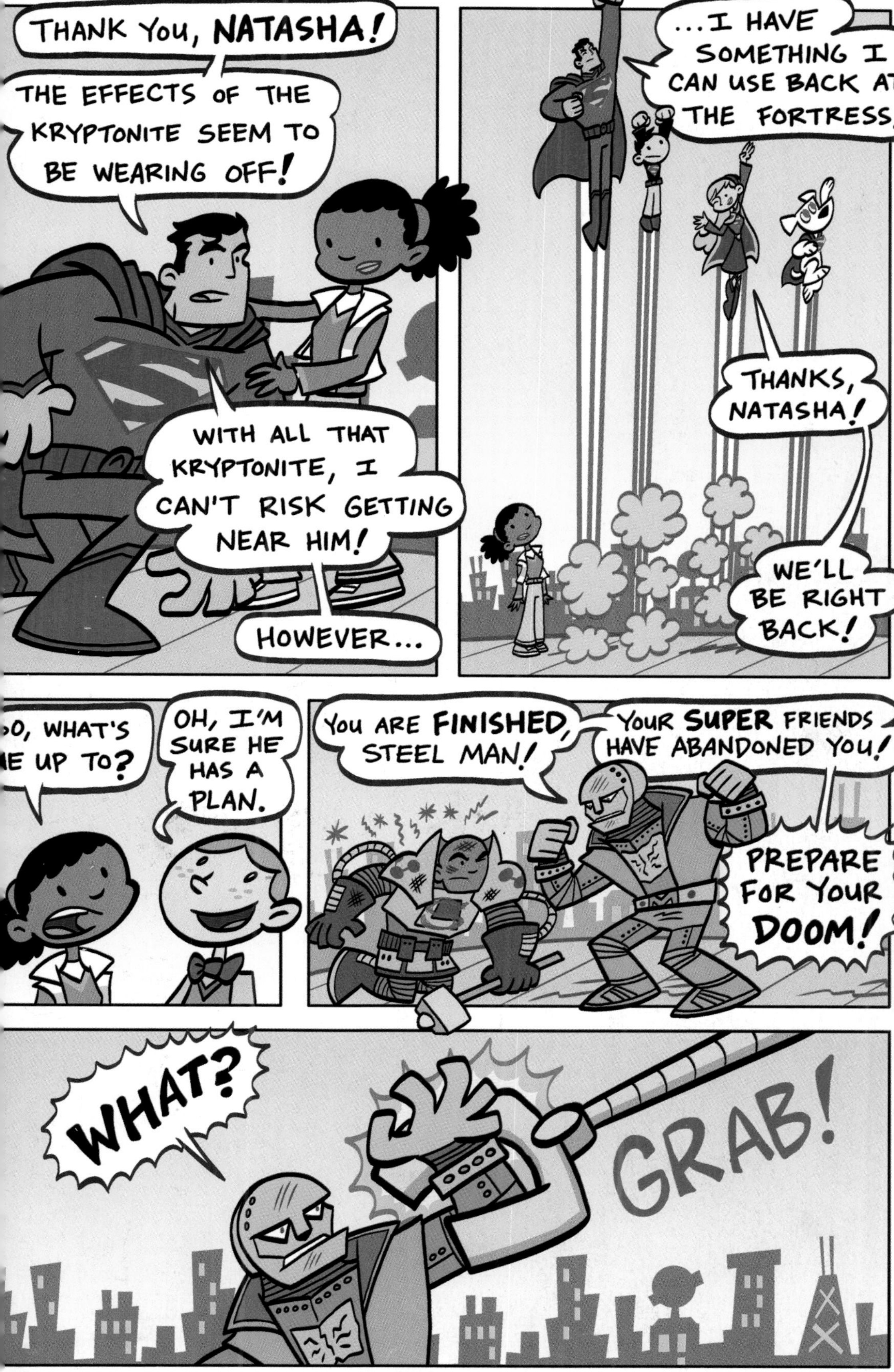
THANK YOU, NATASHA!
THE EFFECTS OF THE KRYPTONITE SEEM TO BE WEARING OFF!
WITH ALL THAT KRYPTONITE, I CAN'T RISK GETTING NEAR HIM!
HOWEVER...
...I HAVE SOMETHING I CAN USE BACK AT THE FORTRESS!
THANKS, NATASHA!
WE'LL BE RIGHT BACK!
O, WHAT'S E UP TO?
OH, I'M SURE HE HAS A PLAN.
YOU ARE FINISHED, STEEL MAN!
YOUR SUPER FRIENDS HAVE ABANDONED YOU!
PREPARE FOR YOUR DOOM!
WHAT?
GRAB!

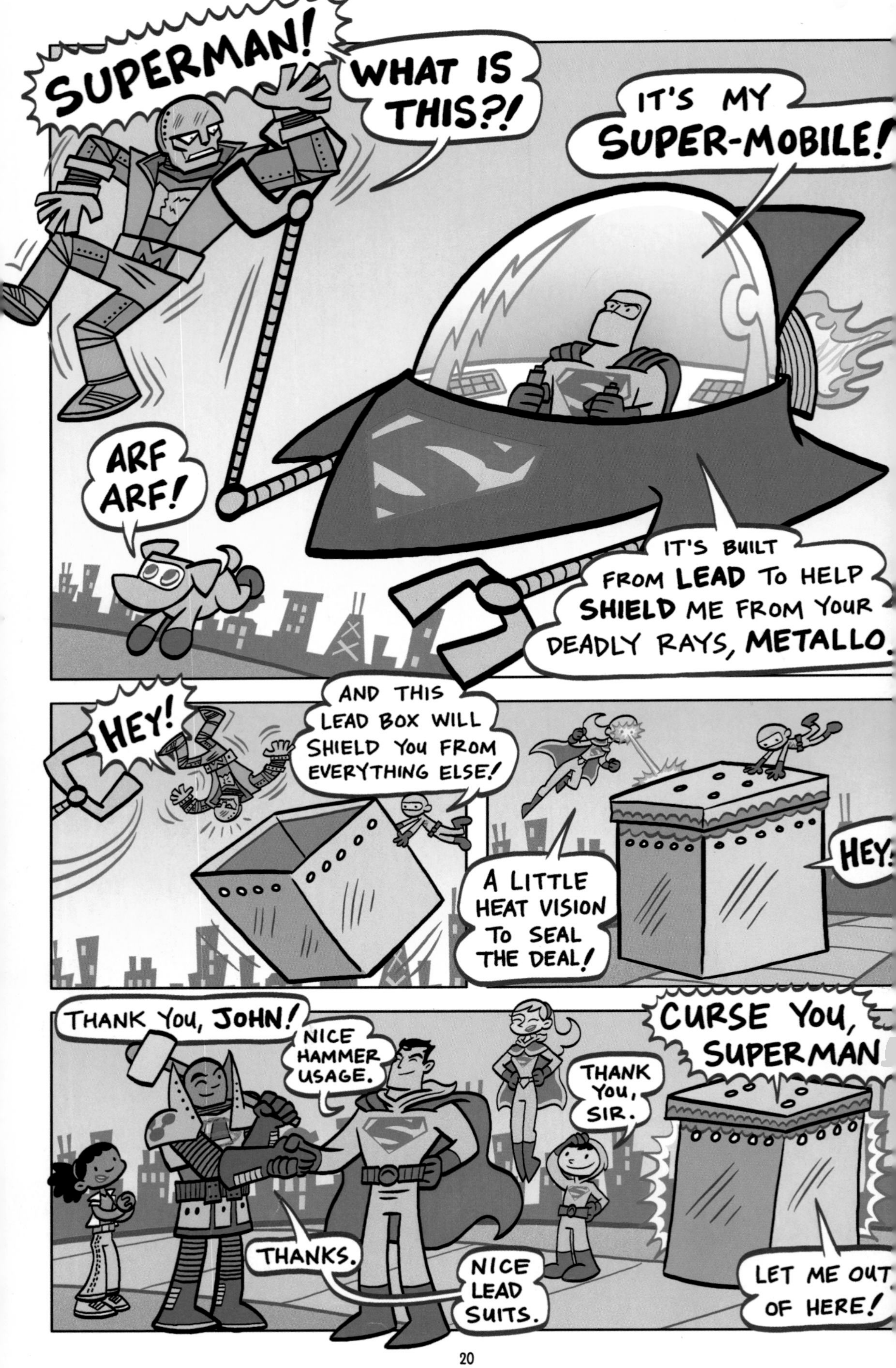
SUPERMAN!
WHAT IS THIS?!
IT'S MY SUPER-MOBILE!
ARF ARF!
IT'S BUILT FROM LEAD TO HELP SHIELD ME FROM YOUR DEADLY RAYS, METALLO.
HEY!
AND THIS LEAD BOX WILL SHIELD YOU FROM EVERYTHING ELSE!
A LITTLE HEAT VISION TO SEAL THE DEAL!
HEY!
THANK YOU, JOHN!
NICE HAMMER USAGE.
THANKS.
NICE LEAD SUITS.
THANK YOU, SIR.
CURSE YOU, SUPERMAN!
LET ME OUT OF HERE!

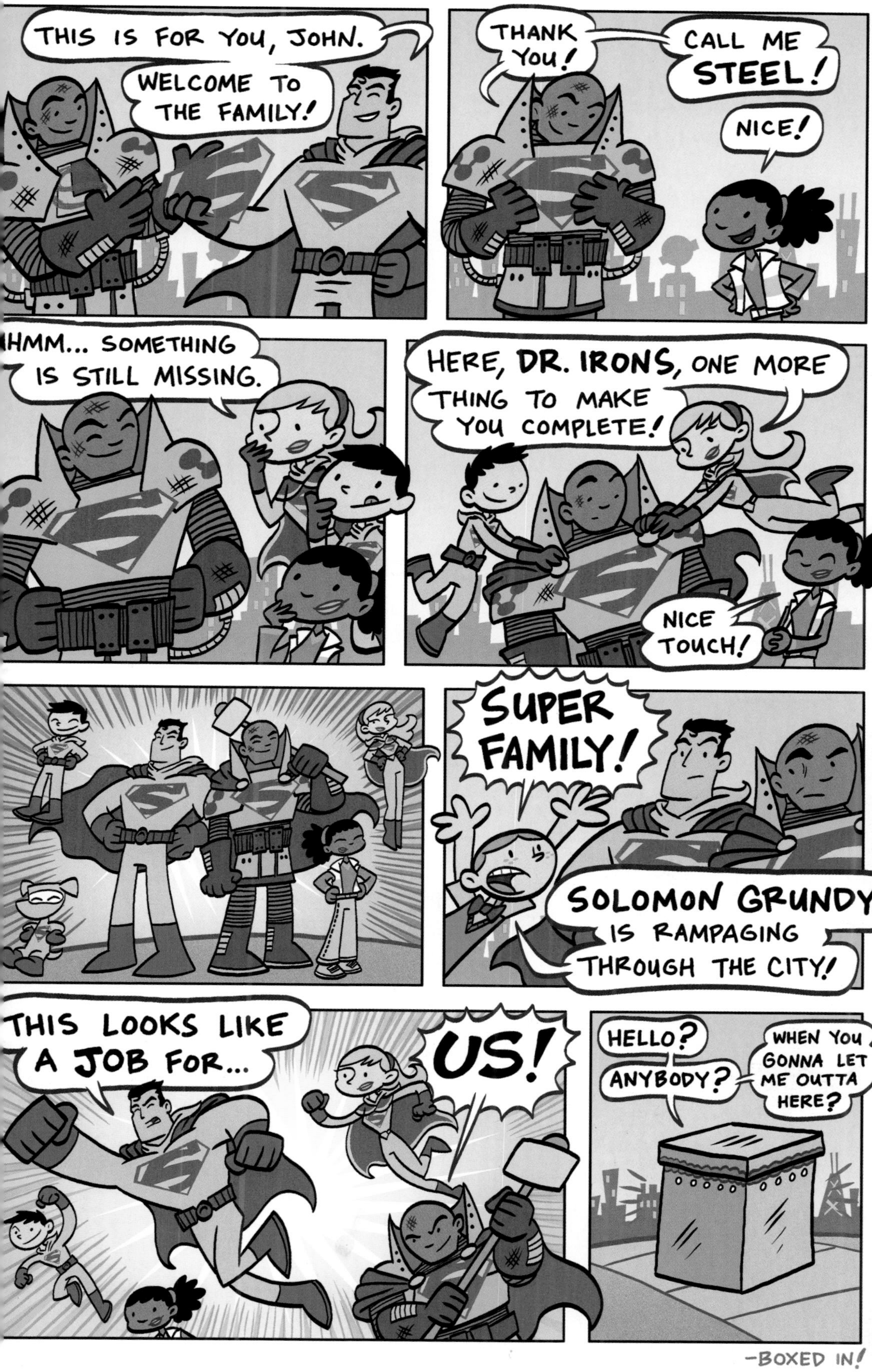
THIS IS FOR YOU, JOHN.
WELCOME TO THE FAMILY!
THANK YOU!
CALL ME STEEL!
NICE!
HMM... SOMETHING IS STILL MISSING.
HERE, DR. IRONS, ONE MORE THING TO MAKE YOU COMPLETE!
NICE TOUCH!
SUPER FAMILY!
SOLOMON GRUNDY IS RAMPAGING THROUGH THE CITY!
THIS LOOKS LIKE A JOB FOR...
US!
HELLO?
ANYBODY?
WHEN YOU GONNA LET ME OUTTA HERE?

-BOXED IN!

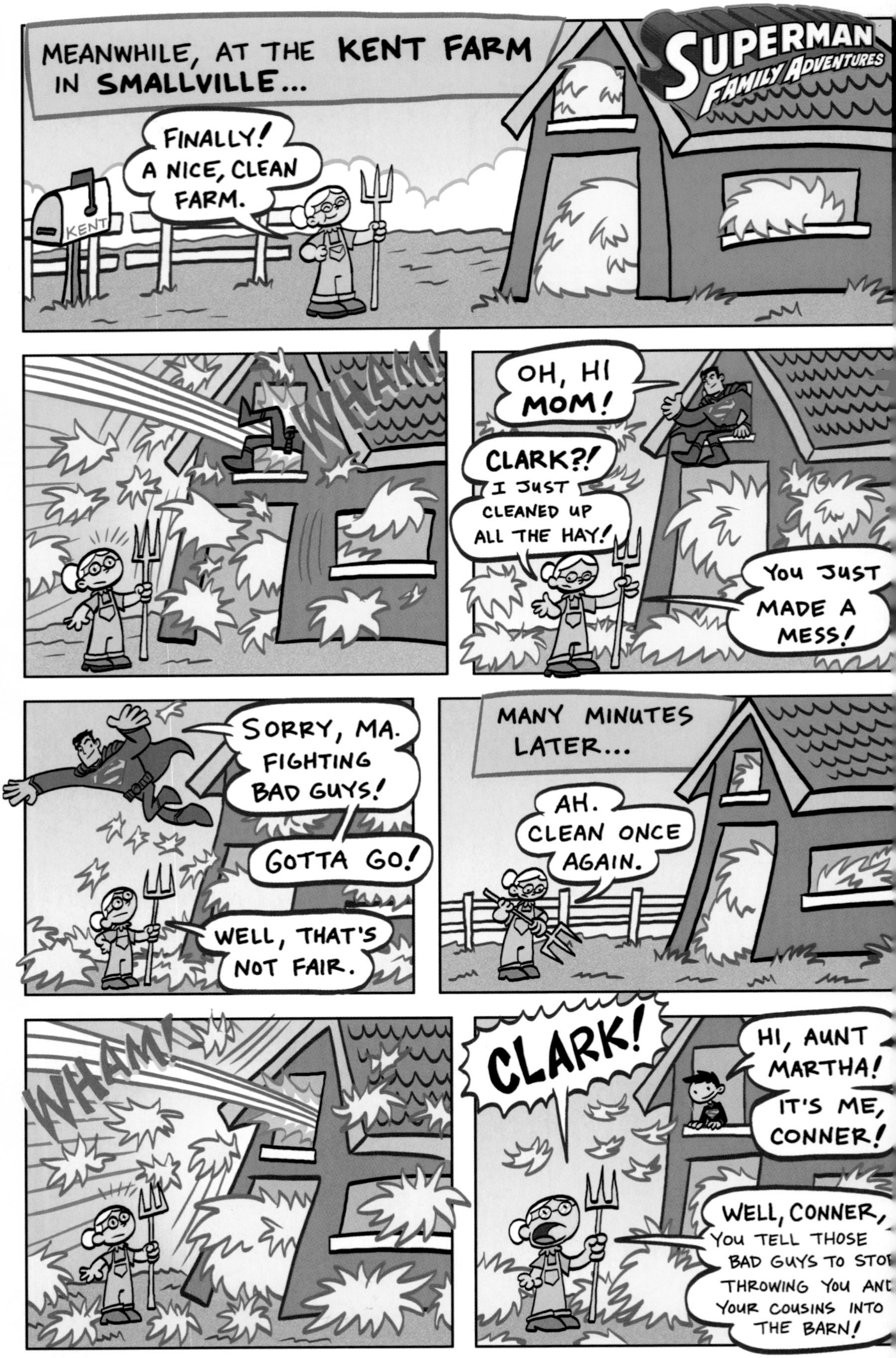
SUPERMAN FAMILY ADVENTURES
MEANWHILE, AT THE KENT FARM IN SMALLVILLE...
KENT
FINALLY! A NICE, CLEAN FARM.
WHAM!
OH, HI MOM!
CLARK?! I JUST CLEANED UP ALL THE HAY!
YOU JUST MADE A MESS!
SORRY, MA. FIGHTING BAD GUYS!
GOTTA GO!
WELL, THAT'S NOT FAIR.
MANY MINUTES LATER...
AH. CLEAN ONCE AGAIN.
WHAM!
CLARK!
HI, AUNT MARTHA!
IT'S ME, CONNER!
WELL, CONNER, YOU TELL THOSE BAD GUYS TO STOP THROWING YOU AND YOUR COUSINS INTO THE BARN!

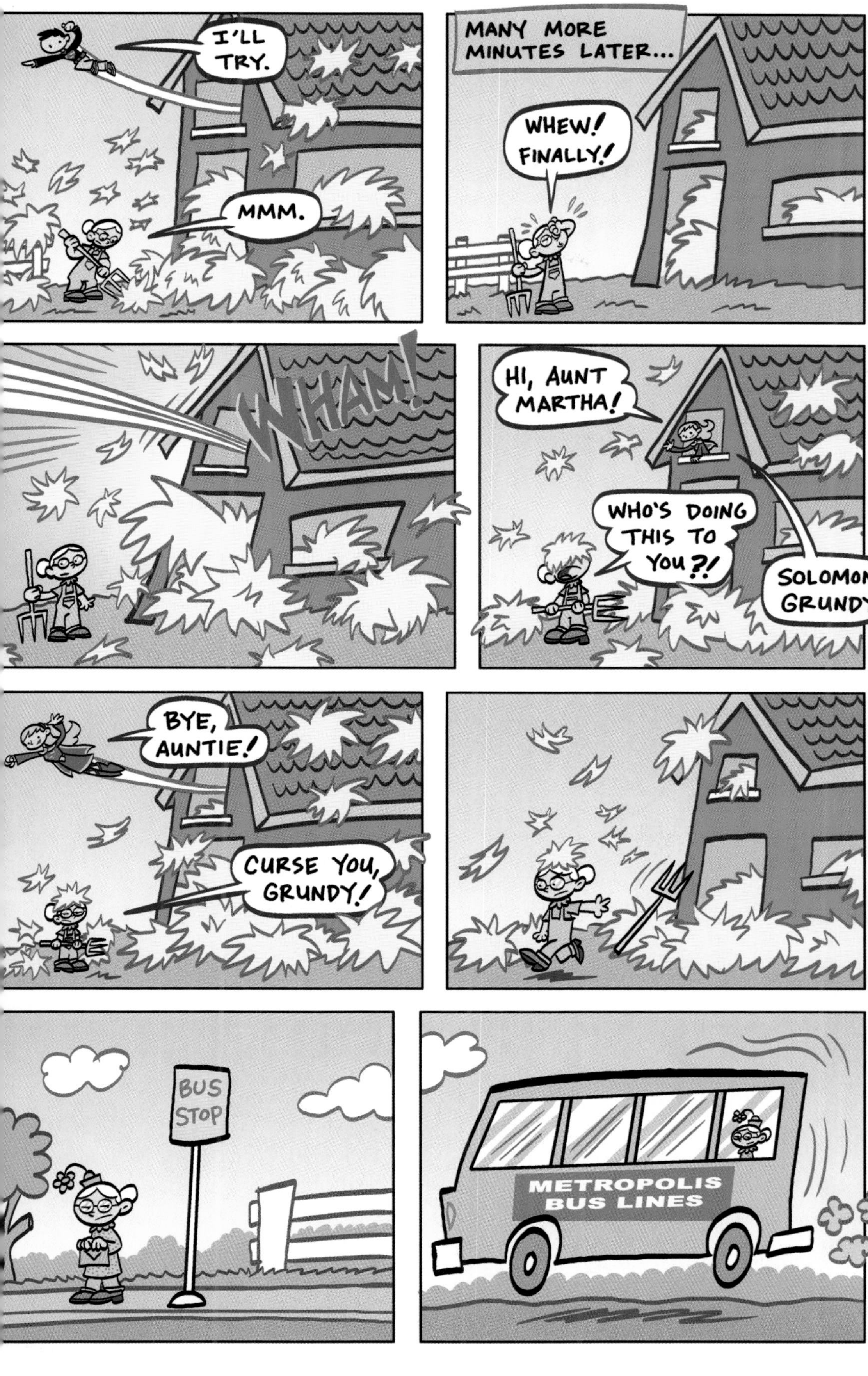
I'LL TRY.
MMM.
MANY MORE MINUTES LATER...
WHEW! FINALLY!
WHAM!
HI, AUNT MARTHA!
WHO'S DOING THIS TO YOU?!
SOLOMON GRUNDY.
BYE, AUNTIE!
CURSE YOU, GRUNDY!
BUS STOP
METROPOLIS BUS LINES

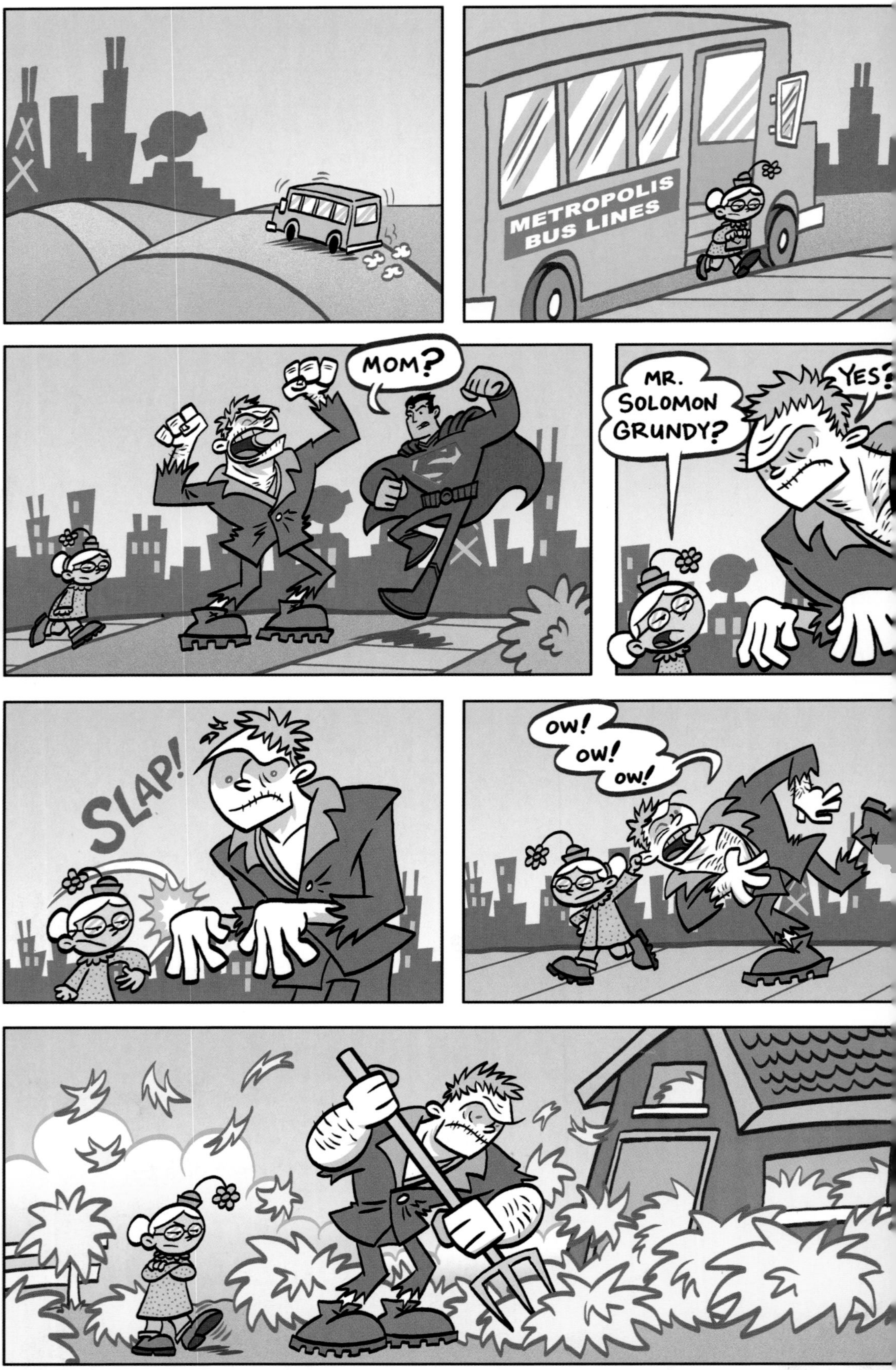
METROPOLIS
BUS LINES
MOM?
MR. SOLOMON GRUNDY?
YES?
SLAP!
OW! OW! OW!

—DEFINITELY NOT A MONDAY.

GLOSSARY

abandoned (uh-BAN-duhnd)—gave up or left forever

analysis (uh-NAL-uh-siss)— an examination of a whole to discover its elements and their relations

armor (AR-mur)—covering worn by soldiers to protect them in battle

asteroid (ASS-tuh-roid)—a small planetoid that travels around the sun

collision (kuh-LIZH-uhn)—the act or instance of crashing together

forcefully, often at high speeds

data (DAY-tuh)—information, or facts

fiery (FYE-uh-ree)—hot or glowing like a fire

fortress (FOR-triss)—a place that is strengthened against attack

fused (FYOOZD)—joined by melting together

genius (JEEN-yuhss)—an unusually smart or talented person

lead (LED)—a soft, gray metal

lousy (LAU-zee)—somewhat ill

meddling (MED-uhl-ing)—interfering in someone else's business

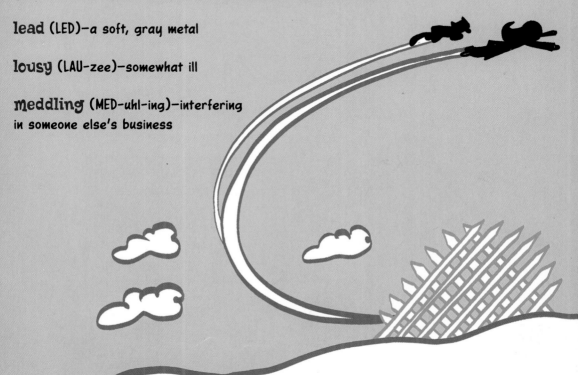

VISUAL QUESTIONS & PROMPTS

1. WHY DO YOU THINK LEX LUTHOR'S SYMBOL WAS FOUND ON JACK CORBEN'S SPACESHIP? EXPLAIN YOUR ANSWER USING EXAMPLES FROM THE STORY.

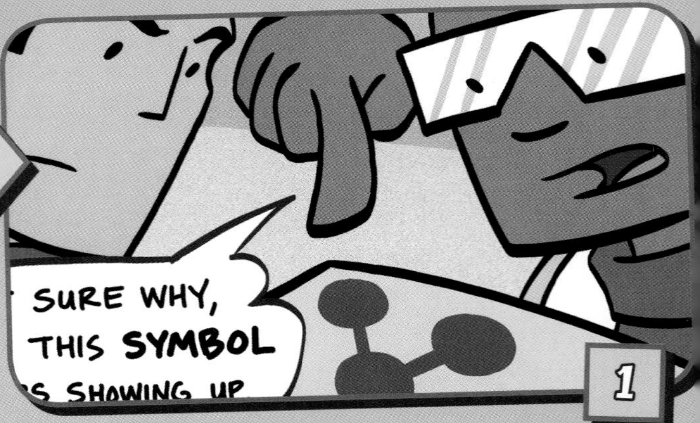
SURE WHY,
THIS SYMBOL
1

2. WHY DO YOU THINK THE ILLUSTRATOR CHOSE TO COLOR JACK CORBEN GREEN IN THE PANEL AT RIGHT?

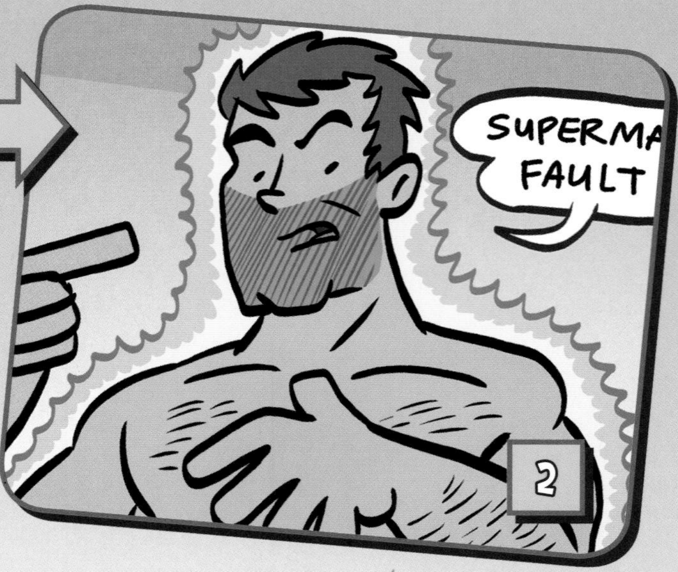
FAULT
2

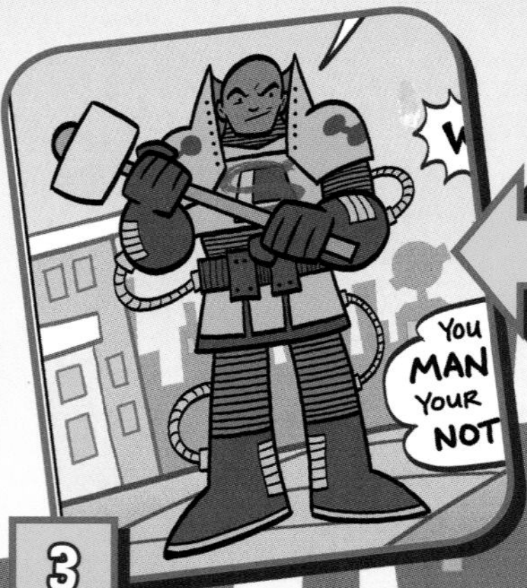
YOU
YOUR
3

3. AT THE END OF THE STORY, JOHN HENRY IRONS BECOMES STEEL, A NEW MEMBER OF THE SUPERMAN FAMILY. WRITE A STORY ABOUT HOW YOU WILL BECOME THE NEXT MEMBER OF THE SUPERMAN FAMILY, AND THEN DRAW A PICTURE OF YOUR UNIFORM.

4. COMIC BOOK ILLUSTRATORS DRAW MOTION LINES (ALSO KNOWN AS ACTION LINES) TO SHOW MOVEMENT OF A CHARACTER OR AN OBJECT, LIKE SUPERMAN FLYING THROUGH THE SKY. FIND OTHER PANELS IN THIS BOOK WITH MOTION LINES. DO YOU THINK THEY MAKE THE ILLUSTRATIONS MORE EXCITING? WHY OR WHY NOT?

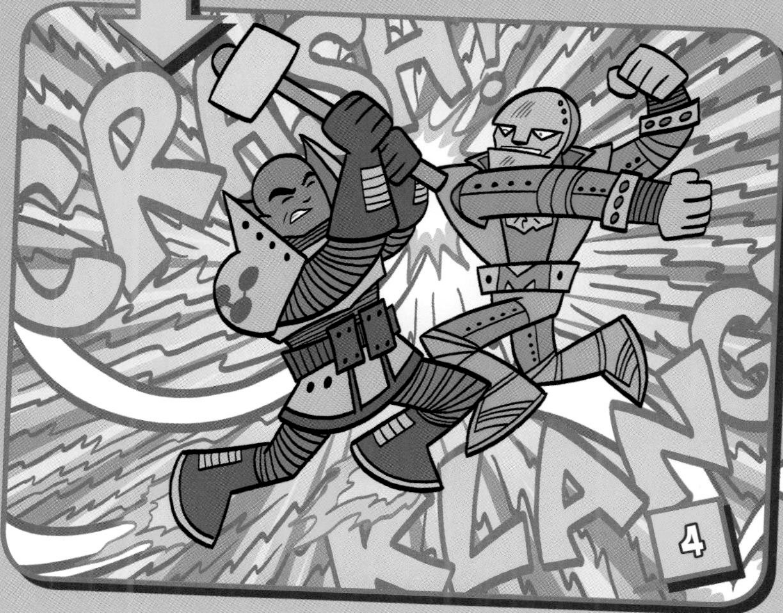
4

5. DO YOU THINK SUPERMAN AND HIS FRIENDS COULD HAVE DEFEATED METALLO WITHOUT LEAD SUITS? WHY OR WHY NOT?

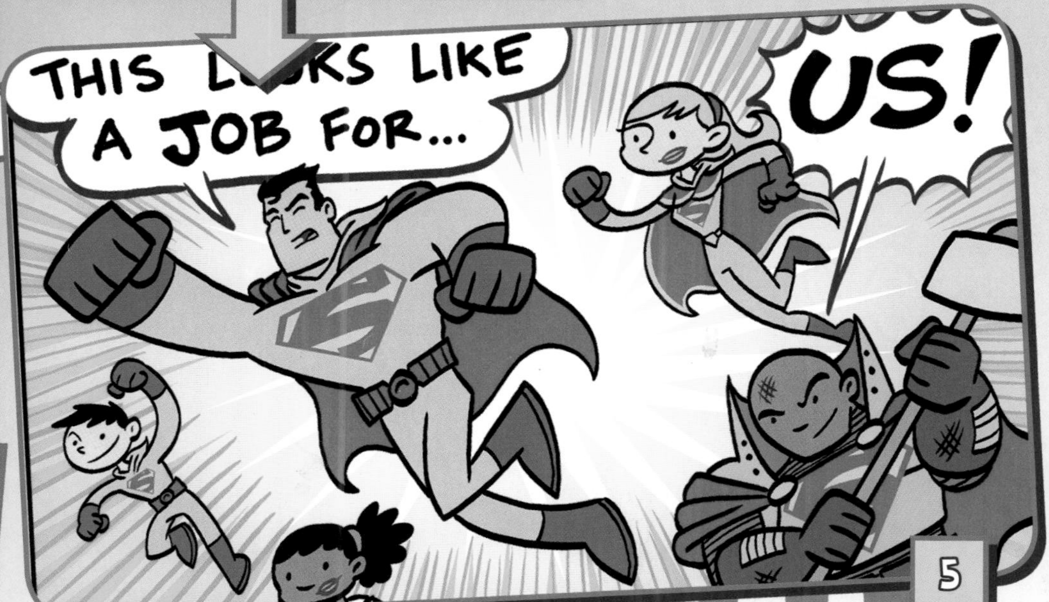
A JOB FOR...
US!
5

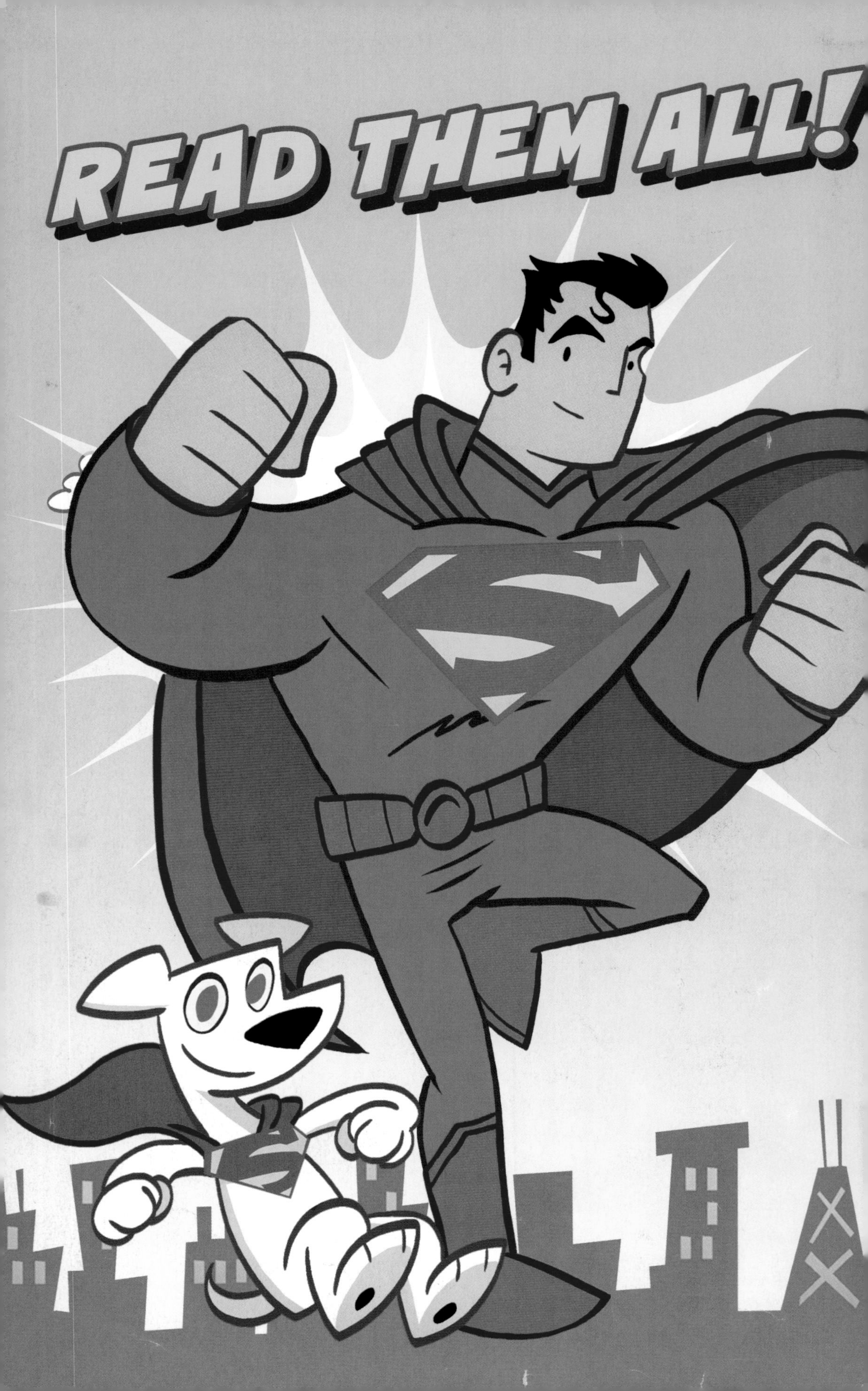
READ THEM ALL!

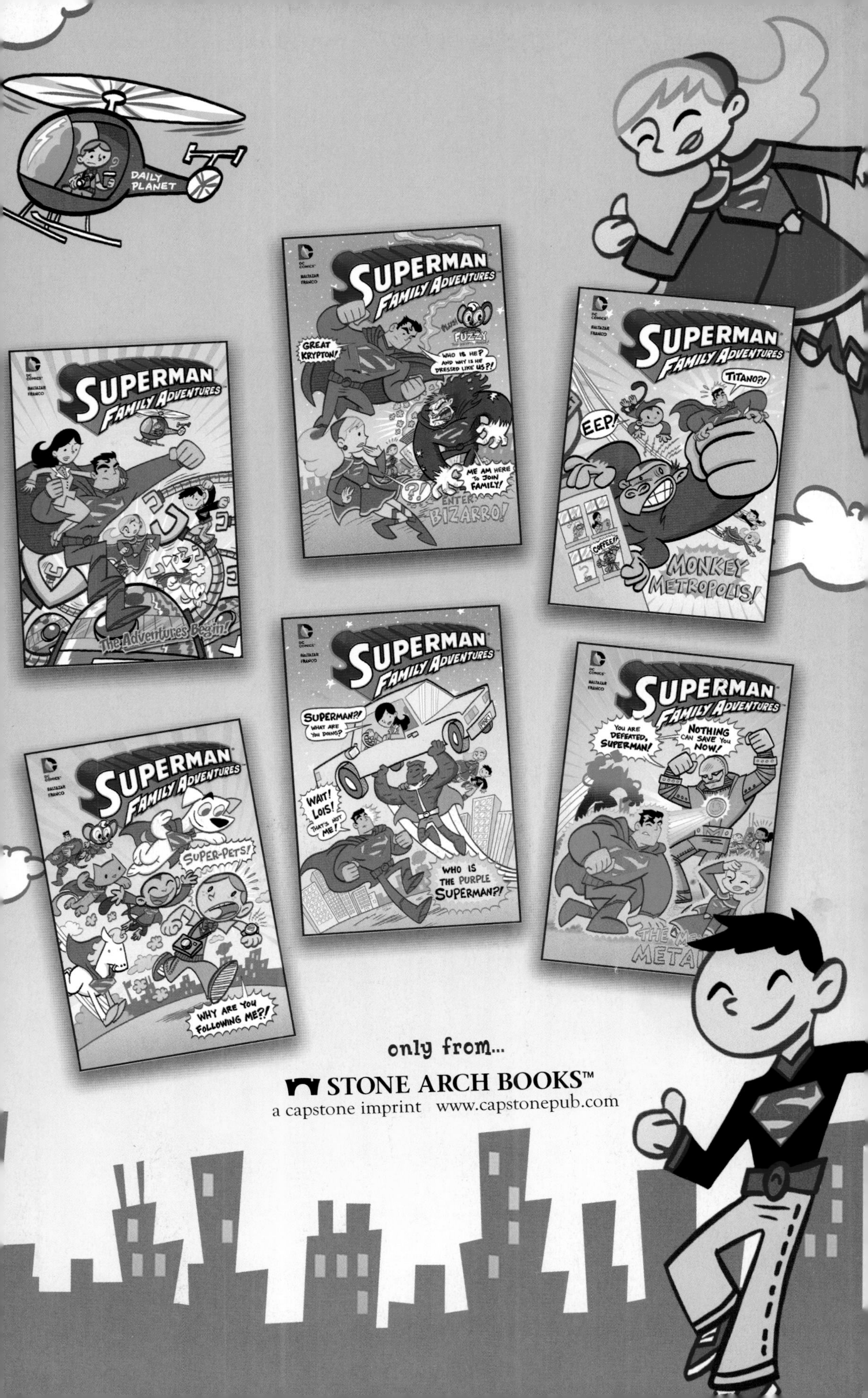
DAILY PLANET
SUPERMAN FAMILY ADVENTURES
The Adventures Begin!
GREAT KRYPTON!
WHO IS HE? AND WHY IS HE DRESSED LIKE US?!
ME AM HERE TO JOIN FAMILY!
ENTER: BIZARRO!
EEP!
TITANO?!
COFFEE!?
MONKEY METROPOLIS!
SUPERMAN?! WHAT ARE YOU DOING?
WAIT! LOIS! THAT'S NOT ME!
WHO IS THE PURPLE SUPERMAN?!
YOU ARE DEFEATED, SUPERMAN!
NOTHING CAN SAVE YOU NOW!
SUPER-PETS!
WHY ARE YOU FOLLOWING ME?!
only from...
STONE ARCH BOOKS™
a capstone imprint www.capstonepub.com

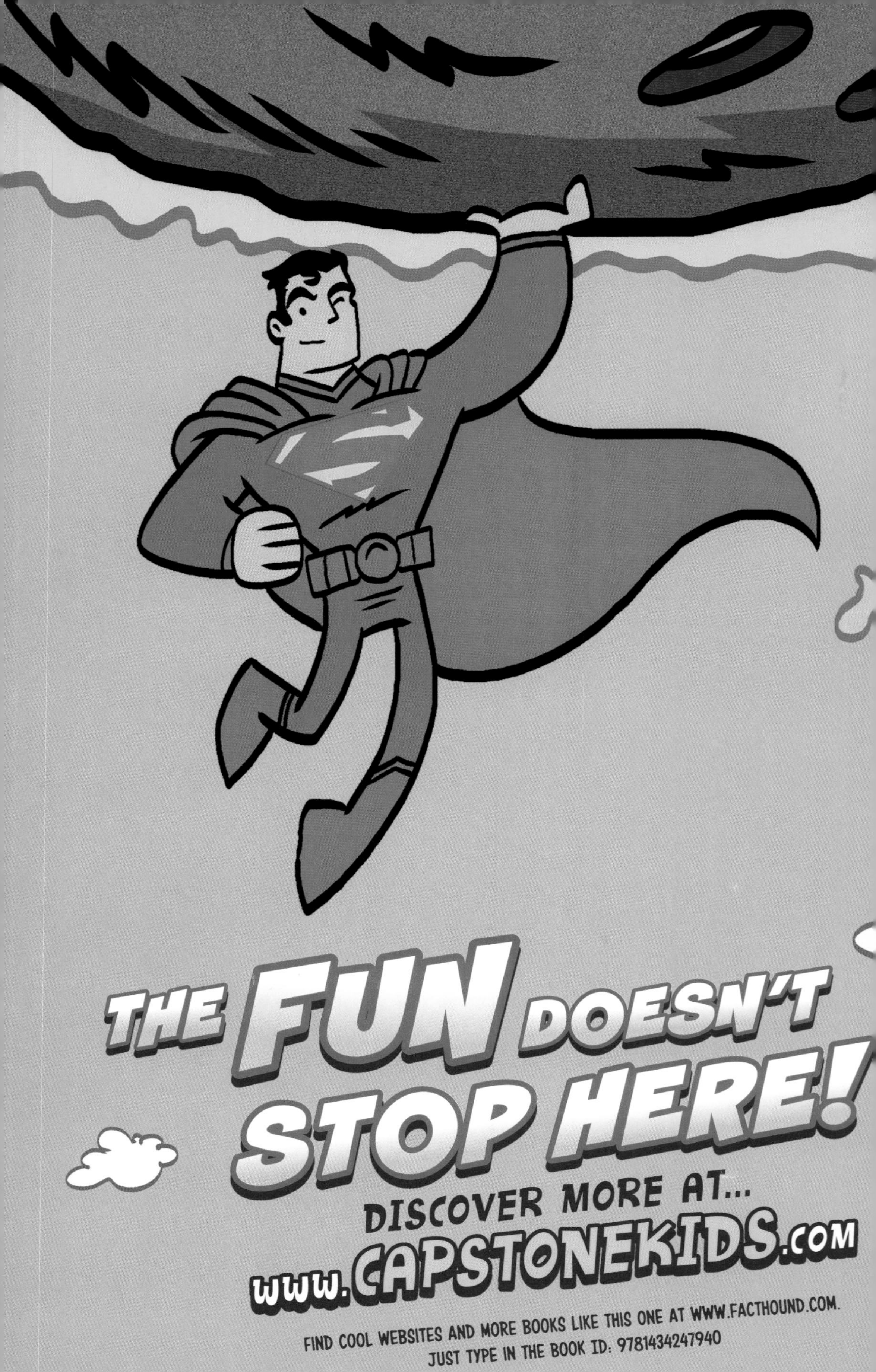